TEARS OF A BROKEN HEART

ELIZABETH PERKINS

Gotham Books

30 N Gould St.
Ste. 20820, Sheridan, WY 82801
https://gothambooksinc.com/

Phone: 1 (307) 464-7800

© 2024 *Elizabeth Perkins*. All rights reserved.

No part of this book may be reproduced, stored in a retrieval system, or transmitted by any means without the written permission of the author.

Published by Gotham Books (June 18, 2024)

ISBN: 979-8-88775-600-4 (P)
ISBN: 979-8-88775-601-1 (E)

Because of the dynamic nature of the Internet, any web addresses or links contained in this book may have changed since publication and may no longer be valid.

The views expressed in this work are solely those of the author and do not necessarily reflect the views of the publisher, and the publisher hereby disclaims any responsibility for them.

TABLE OF CONTENTS

Obituary i
Note from the Elizabeth v
Tears of a Broken Heart 1
Friday 12
Saturday 17
Sunday 23
Monday 25
Tuesday 34
Criminal Law & Procedure 35
Double Jeopardy 36
Burdens of Proof and Burden-Shifting Statutes 37
Wednesday 40
Thursday 41
Friday 45
Saturday 50
Sunday 60
Just For You 67
Monday 71
Brandon's Words July 20, 2016 108
The Waves of Missing You 110

OBITUARY

Brandon Lamar Holmes came into this world October 5, 1986 to Curtis and Marchelle at Christina Hospital in Newark Delaware. He was the most beautiful baby in the hospital ward. All the nurses adored him and continuously doted on him. Brandon was everything his father said he would be. And once we left the hospital for home. His father held him up to the open sky and said: Behold the only thing better than yourself. There were so many stars in the sky that night.

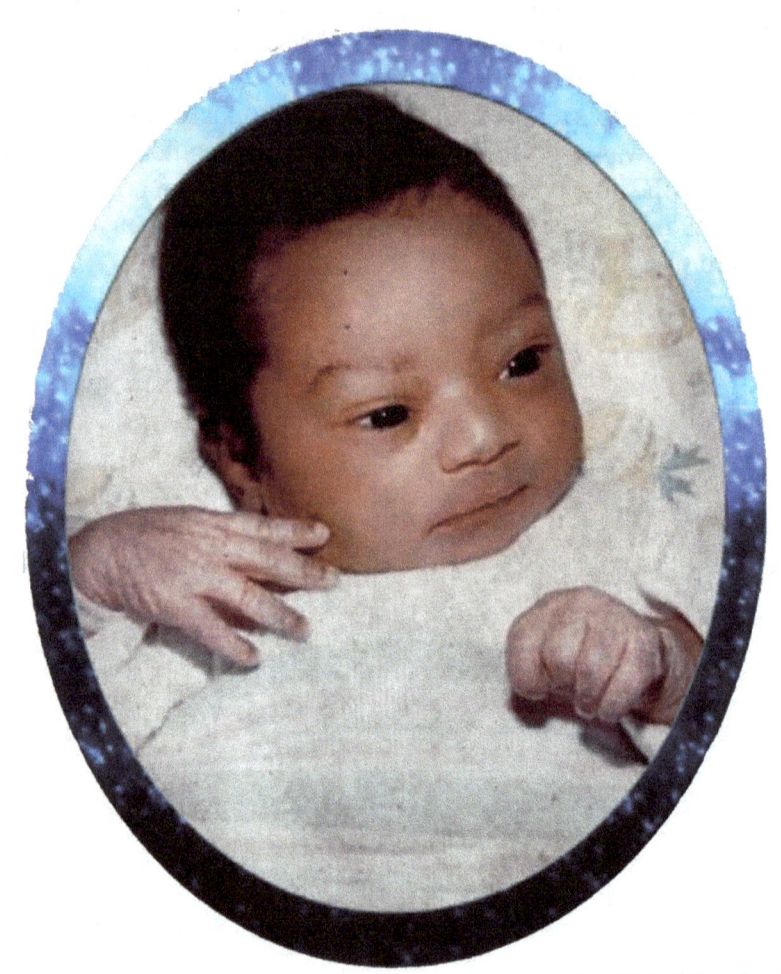

Brandon L Holmes

TEARS OF A BROKEN HEART

Lamar

Brandon attended William Penn High School and he studied Criminal Law and graduated in 2004 but singing was his passion (Mar) we lovingly called was an incredible singer and did several events here in his hometown Wilmington Delaware. In 2006, Brandon was blessed to conceive a daughter Leasia. He was a doting father and still wanted more so he tried out for American Idol but he didn't make it because they were looking for something different in a singer for that show.

ELIZABETH PERKINS

Brandon then tried his hand in modeling though they wanted him his mind was on his music and going to college to pass the Bar.

NOTE FROM THE ELIZABETH

I started writing this book because I wanted to write something steamy and my thought was a sex man working his way to the top. A self-made man. Working a real job and pushing his way through college. But it had to be a job that he didn't like and didn't want anyone to know who he was. Not in college studying criminal law, that would surely not look good with his professors. You see I always think from a woman's point of view but what that of a man. I can only think from a woman point of view and I can't think from a man's point of view so who can I find to fill this male character and bring realism to this book. I had one person in mind: he can sing dance and he is very handsome. And that would be my son Brandon Holmes.

Thinking back to where I came from...Always wondered what it would be like becoming the man I am today. Had a lot of falls to get up from...had a lot of pressure to release and had a lot of anger to let go... I'm still learning and love the fact that I have meet The Father. He is known to me as any person I see in front of me (Thank you Lord for not giving up on me) Thank you for your constant reminders of my blessings. Thank you for my family and our strength. I love you Jesus...you are forever my savoir. God bless everyone.

People are so happy to break or hurt someone, just watching their pain brings a smile to your face.... the world is full of sick people and when I see these murders, kidnappings of children and then all these dumb ass people talking of how funny it is to see a guy/girl getting played or disrespected makes me sick. What if today was your last...? Would you be happy

ELIZABETH PERKINS

with the life you lived? Try doing something that's hard to do like... Making people happy and making great changes in your life that's not going to damage someone else. I'm not above no one nor am I beneath no one. Change should start today.

TEARS OF A BROKEN HEART

My days are dark... and life gets harder...I see no light at the end of the tunnel...I feel like I'm a goner... what do you do when there is no one to save you? There was nothing great about me to speak of me. Judging from my history I've realize that I'm not the man you once knew. I've learned a lot from the past years and continue to rise above myself every day. I love me more now than I ever did before. I thank God for these changes in me... for without him I would be lost. Gone into the darkness... My Princess and I await the sun to shine on us once more. For the beauty of the ones smile may bring us forever joy and happiness.

Brandon opened his eyes turning over to see a beautiful young girl sleeping next to him, he sighs to himself: I'm tired of this shit. He gets up out of bed to put on his sweats when he hears...

Hey baby, what time is it? A woman asked.

Brandon turns towards her saying: just leave ok...he walks into the bathroom to take a shower; all his anguish was visible on his face as his tears were washed away by the warm water, Flashbacks of memories of a bitter past (May 26, 2010) Brandon was laid back in his king-sized sanctuary, his eyes closed, and his body was in a prolonged state of excitement.

What could he have possibly have done right to be honored by the presence of his Nubian goddess, whose exquisite honey brown body is blissfully draped across his chest? His arm is draped around her delicate brown shoulder, firmly holding her close, despite the fact that he fears nothing; he can't bear the thought of losing her. They lay there together, neither of them asleep, basking in the pure love that they have for each other. Brandon moves his outstretched arm down her shoulder to meet the sweet curve at the small of her back, and strokes her gently across her beautifully rounded bottom.

Her cheeks quiver ever so slightly as he gently caressed her soft sweet flesh, and with that she slowly draped her leg across him in a way that tells him she doesn't want him to move from that spot. With a free hand, he brushes the hair away from her lovely face as she looks up at him with her lovely brown eyes. He was moved to hold her closer to him, and she responds by slowly pushing her hot womanhood against his thigh, Brandon could feel the moisture of her inner woman trickle down his leg. He felt her hips quiver, and she closed her eyes and kisses him on his chest. Then he felt the heat welling up within them both, and he move to pull her closer still. She brushed her lips across his nipple, and then, in a move that surged through him in a wave of pure joy, she bit him gently and moaned in such a sweet voice.

Brandon wanted her on top of him right then, and she must have read his thoughts, because before he could move her body one inch, she was on top of him, guiding him inside of her, her eyes half closed, her mouth half open, and that unmistakable fire sweeping through them both. They made sweet love until they were hot and sweaty, both breathing heavily. Before he got up, he took a long look and his queen thinking: if something was to happen to her he thought as he grabbed a towel; there were so many girls in my past that I watched do some of the worst things to themselves. I mean beautiful girls with great bodies that got caught up in the fast life of stripping and jumping from guy to guy. I look at some of them today and can't believe how that damaged has changed their life completely. And they are no way near where they are supposed

TEARS OF A BROKEN HEART

to be. Why do beautiful women act so trashy and nasty? And crave the wrong attention that is already given freely.

You see Brandon was an entertainer at a club called Ever-Quest, it was a Thursday night (The Ultimate Girls Night Out!) and the club was filling with eager women that have been waiting for this exhilarating production. The flyer read:

Welcome to the Quest providing fantastic exotic temptations with style. Husbands and boyfriends beware! The show is completely raw with multiple opportunities for intimate audience participation. Choreographed and created with one goal in mind, the pleasure of women: That evening would be a great turn of events for Brandon.

Marcel: Got it. I'll get Demi to the club, and maintain the surprise. Trust I'll avoid Charley like the plague.

Great I've got Danny here with me putting all gifts in the car as we speak, we even got a piñata stuffed with all kinds of sweet erotic oils like vanilla dream and some of her favorite facial mask Velour Cooter spritz that make you smell like chocolate sprinkles. You know she has a thing for things with taste she laughs, and then were headed over to Hollies to prep for Demi's birthday party before we met up at the club.

Great I better get going before I miss Demi, wouldn't want her leaving the house without me.

She arrived at Demi's house at 3:30pm when she knocked on the door Demi opened the door with Noxzema on her face. Yikes! Either I'm at the wrong house or I missed Halloween she laughed.

You're so funny Marcel, come on in. What are you doing here I didn't expect anyone to come over today?

ELIZABETH PERKINS

Are you kidding it's your birthday!

Yeah, I know but I was going to spend it alone.

Why? Is something wrong?

Well Charley is still blowing up my phone driving me the hell crazy, he doesn't get the message that it's over.

Well, the next time he calls just answer it and tell him to stop calling you.

I don't know, I'm so over him.

Good and if I'm wrong, I'll be right beside you for moral support. Look Demi I love you, but at some point, you just have to rip off the band aid with some people. Her phone rings: Hello. What?! Oh my god! I'll be there in one hour!

What's going on?!

Holly's car won't start, and she stuck in Philly. She said she's parked by some club called Everquest and its getting dark so come get her because the streets are full of unsavory people at night.

Man, bummer.

Are you having serious déjà vu right now?

Well, you know Philadelphia doesn't get a lot of love these days.

Whoa. That was harsh Demi. Everybody loves hanging out in Philly.

Uh yeah, if you say so…

TEARS OF A BROKEN HEART

Ahh, I'll have to catch up with you later, I guess. That is unless you want to ride with; I would hate to take that ride alone at this time. Besides you're not doing anything else.

I guess you'd know.

Whoa, easy. No need to freak out, tell you what. After we pick up Holly, we can celebrate your birthday. Come on...

Demi couldn't believe her friends didn't plan anything for her birthday and she thought it to be too much to remind them since they always did something for each other's birthday every year. But Holly was in a bind with her car, so we might as well go help her. Surly she would do the same for her is she was in trouble. On the ride Charley was still calling her phone.

Marcel: You know you really should think about what part you play in the breakup of your relationship.

Demi: I'm sure Charley it is telling everyone I'm such a bad person. And that's fine he can say whatever he likes, I really don't care. Hey, I wasn't the one letting all and everyone into our relationship and I defiantly wasn't telling all our business to everyone on my job and showing off every chance I got to look like I was doing more then what was really going on. Every time I went to pick him up here comes somebody following him out to meet me. "Talkin bout I heard a lot about you." And I would smile and say really, looking at him.

When I said something about it he would say: I didn't tell them nothing, they just followed me out here. Why is he always complaining to these fools at his job? I continually talked with him about it, but he doesn't hear anything I say, I mean what's up with guys like this? Sooo I would just drive on and turn the music up until we got to our destination, which is usually Fridays. Once inside he would again try to show out for whomever and be all over me, pulling and grabbing trying to kiss me. It was disgusting, like he never had a girlfriend before. I would push him away and the look on my face and my body language spoke for itself.

The Maître-D would seat us, and he would get up and come sit down in my seat with me. I'm like "oh no you don't you go sit back over there, that's why they make the seating like this. So, I can look at you and you can look at me and talk looking eye to eye." He was so stupid and needy, never giving me my space and just crowding me. When the waiter came to take our order, I would immediately ask for a long island ice tea. He would order a coke soda as usual, then I would order the 10 oz sirloin steak cooked medium rare with a rack of baby back ribs falling off the bone, basted in Tennessee barbeque sauce with side orders of mashed potatoes and broccoli cooked soft. He would order a Hamburger as always, I mean nothing ever changed with this guy and he would try to sound so cool saying things like "I would kill somebody over you". I didn't think that was cool at all, it was all so annoying and sure he worked but he was the kind of guy that would tell his mama's business and she was dead. Not to mention his crying fits about nothing, he would over think something and just start crying like for what?

After a while I broke up with him over a text because I really didn't want to talk to him face to face. Sometimes leaving is easy for some people and sometimes it hurts to know the love you thought you had was slowly fading away. He was so pathetic, good thing I never had sex with him or even kissed him. Ugh shudder the thought… He became a stalker and would just continuously call my phone for like half a summer, so I had my phone turned off for like two weeksto get him to stop all together and just forget about me. Then when I had turned it back on, this fool was still calling me and now Holly's car is on the brink on my birthday, what kind of cruel universe is this?!

Demi and Marcel pull around the corner from the club.

TEARS OF A BROKEN HEART

Marcel: I think this is it.

Where are we? Demi asked.

Marcel: Come on and stop moping, what's wrong with you anyway?

Loud music was coming from inside the building when they walk pass Demi read the marquee:(Sexy exotic dancers!)

Surprise! Marcel yelled.

Marcel: Did you really think for one moment we forgot about your birthday, Girl you gone have a blast. I can't get over the last show they had in New York

Demi: I don't know Marcel I heard some crazy stuff about places like this.

Marcel: You've never been one to shy away from a challenge, besides I just talked to Holly and Sassy they are meeting us inside.

Demi: This is just so unexpected; I thought you guys would have taken me out to a happy hour to celebrate my birthday, not take me to a strip joint.

Just then Sassy walked out the door.

Sassy: You made it. My bff radar was indicating that my services were needed out here.

Marcel: Yeah, Demi is not sure about going in.

Marcel: I know you are not going to stand out here and leave us in there to get our groove on without you, are you?

Sassy: Go inside Marcel holly is at our table, we'll be in, in a few minutes.

Demi: I don't know about this Sassy.

Sassy: Look Demi, it's your birthday and on your birthday, you got to wake up with determination and go to bed with satisfaction.

Demi: What the heck is that supposed to mean?

Sassy: I saw that on a mug at the dollar store and it sounded motivational (she laughed.) Come on, it's going to be great! (Grabbing Demi's hand)

Demi: I'm so nervous; it is cold in here because I'm shaking.

Sassy: Calm down these guys can sense a first timer, it's your birthday girl let your eyes feast on the deliciousness and be happy for a moment!

The girls sat at a table with a fantastic view of the stage, to make sure they had an up close and personal experience with the dancers.

Sassy: Check out that guy.

You could feel the excitement in the air as they sat down. There was a card on the table that read; fantasies will be fulfilled for birthday girls, bachelorettes and women just looking for a good time. Leave your inhibitions at the door. The thrills don't stop with the show itself, the men that turn you on will be in the Flirt Lounge to take pictures with their fans or share a conversation and maybe a laugh or two. The waiter came over to take their order.

TEARS OF A BROKEN HEART

Ladies may I get you something to eat or drink?

Demi looked up, as her eyes rose up to meet his face. She could tell that the night her friends had in store for was sure to be a good one. This man is beautiful, beefy, had her at a loss for words and the only thing escaped her lips was…

Demi: Uh huh, name?

He smiled warmly at her…

They call me Lamar (he couldn't tell her his government name) and what can I get you ladies?

Her best friend Marcel answered…

Marcel: Sex on the beach would be real nice…

Sassy: Ooh girl (as they start laughing) sex on the beach for all of us Lamar.

Bartender: (The bartender calls over) what you need Lamar?

He walks over to the bar; sex on the beach table for 4.

Bartender: It's gone be a busy night.

Yeah, and it's about to get even busier (as he hands him the order form) take care of that for me.

Bartender: Got cha...

The MC announced: good evening, ladies! Thank you all so much for your love and support of our show. We'd like to pleasure you with the sensationalism of Lamar! This man is looking for a lady that's classy with a wild side, his guilty pleasure is eating mangos, but he never met an ice cream flavor he didn't like!

Queuing up the music his body moved slowly across the floor, grinding up and down with the motion of the snake. His eyes were strategically focused on the women in the audience. Demi watched in amazement while her body was responding to his movement, she began to get hot as he danced his movements played with her imagination. The seductive spotlight was on her table being that she was one of the birthday girls at the show. The women cheered during his high-energy performance. He playfully engaged his female audience members as he acted out the ladies' fantasies.

Demi had him on her mind bad while receiving his energy, and she could not resist sending him a note on a napkin when she saw him grinding in his performance. The note read (I love the way you danced can I buy you a drink or some wine?) Brandon smiled toward the jester. Then he heard his friend say, you can gimme that if you're not going to make use of it? Brandon tossed the note in the trash mumbling to his-self (women)

Christen: The cats are scratching tonight man you better jump on that.

Brandon tells him: You know Christen its only room for one dog around here and I got to bounce man…Early morning.

Christen: I hear that. Tell you what…I'll save you some (he starts laughing)

Brandon wasn't just a dancer he was a Business Major at University of Delaware he was an intelligent mind and determined to pass the bar. And not the one where people where drinking. Women wanted him any way they could get him, anytime they could get him. He was very comprehensive about

TEARS OF A BROKEN HEART

dating because he wanted more out of life, so he stayed focused on his task in this life.

FRIDAY

Friday nights were crazy with so many women pulling at him and the other dancers, throwing money like it was the last stand and the women loved having their way while fulfilling their mental fantasies for attention and affection that was missing from their bedrooms. The first week of every month was when checks came out and the most money came in. All those lonely single and married women, you know the type that isn't getting it at home and the hubby isn't doing his job right (just making it rain all over the brother).

There were nights when Mister Jody gave private dances, conversation, long hard continuous rides in the flirt room, for some of them god fearing ladies out there... Well let's just say they loved milking our hard bodies in the back room, in the ally by the trash cans and even in the back seat of their cars. They spent their hubby's money like it was water and we were just the tall glass of water they needed to quench their thrust. Right now, I'm a thirsty man choosing my pray for the evening, as I take the stage, I see a familiar face. Taking my time to reach my destination, collecting payment as eye candy for all these horny ass women that wanted to ride me all the way home, my approach is swift. Considering her eyes, I can feel no resistance and she is mine:

Brandon: Can I have this dance?

Demi: No, you dance for me.

She watched him extremely closely and her mind was open; his dance encouraged her body to answer him in rhythms. It's hard to explain what he did to her, but her body will never be the same. She liked his raunchy style and he showed her no mercy, but his shy side made her want to know more about him, the pressure was on as she handed him a fifty-dollar bill whispering; let me buy you that drink Lamar, I promise I won't bite.

Brandon smiled and responded; I don't drink...

Demi: Really, then what do you do?

Brandon: Curious about me, are you?
Demi: Maybe... I know you get asked a lot, right?

Brandon: Uh-huh I do, I get that same question from a lot of women.

She could hear other women tainting her as she took his time (Girl if you don't let him go your going to explode in that chair!) The ladies were taunting and fussing over his time waiting for him to give it to them like he's giving it to her on the floor (come on!) Brandon left Demi so hungry she had to get some water and some air. She could not bring herself to come down from this high she was set upon and she wanted more. As her girls follow her outside.

If I'm considered guilty for what goes on inside my mind, then give me the Electric chair for all my future crimes (she laughs) I listen to too much Prince, which gives me a naturally Dirty Mind.

I'm dirty minded by nature! (She laughs)

Its ok we all get those.

I'm sorry but I just snapped his picture, I'm going get his pictures developed and hang them on my wall!

Oh my! I'm going to need to repent for what I was thinking about that young man.

ELIZABETH PERKINS

Man, it should be a sin to look so delicious. Oops did I say that! They all start laughing, enjoying the moment.

Giiiiiiiirrllll this is what I want for my birthday he was thick and juicy!

Now you know you he shouldn't tease us single women like that; oh my god!

Meanwhile Brandon is changing in the dressing room thinking about how everything he had to do tomorrow, he has the perfect life, he could do everything he wanted and go anywhere he wanted. He was a man on the move and there was nothing in his way to stop him, until I he met (her) coming out if the dressing room Demi's eyes was set on Lamar, he had just walked out of the dressing room for another performance, dressed in ocean blue and looking quite scrumdiliumptious. So, she made her way towards him: excuse me, wow you look unreal; I um mean you never answered me question? I mean you seem so maintained (catching her breath for a moment she said) I'm Demi…

He thought she was very charming and from the first moment he seen her all he could do was smile: You think I'm maintained, that's funny…

Yes… smiling bashfully, let's just say you're different, I mean I sent you a note on a napkin and you didn't respond that was rude of you.

I was being polite.

Really, is that what you're calling it?

Yes, I'm not like these other guys in here; I'm different than you may think sweetheart.

TEARS OF A BROKEN HEART

Curiosity set in: what do you mean?

I do things different then these other berthas in here, that's why I stand out. So, what do you want to know about me?

Before she could even speak her first thoughts was; he's so arrogant and bold I would walk away but instead she said: well, I was wondering. Do you have a girlfriend?

He responds: typical question but no, do you have a man?

She starts to speak: no…?

(The MC's voice called out looking for him Brandon!) you're up man!

Demi looked at him: I thought you said they call you Lamar?

Yeah, they do. He headed back inside as she watched him walk away, but she was totally sold on him thinking: whoever he is fucking I know she is loving that shit! When she walked back to her table, she shared her thoughts with her friends: I am so definitely hooked and addicted…love me some Lamar, for real!

I bet he runs through his house bucket naked!

I would lock your tail in the closet with him.

Demi said not so innocently: Aww, I don't think he would know what to do with me…

Yeah, don't let his quiet demeanor fool you; those are the ones we get strung out on. Slap your ass up rub it down Oh no!!!

Yeah, he probably hasn't had pussy since pussy had him.

ELIZABETH PERKINS

Girl: If a man can't please my cove he can't please me, I got too much freak in me girl. I need a man that knows what he doing Rock is still a child playing in the sand box; Now Christopher can get the business girl…

Yikes!

Speechless! The girls were having a ball.

SATURDAY

Saturday morning Jimmy was working behind the bar there was so much to be done before all the hustle and bustle and running before the night's opening Kareemah walked in (Excuse me do you know when Antonio comes in?) he flirted with her: he won't be in till latter, is there something I could do for you beautiful? Yeah, can you call him for me (she lied) we had an appointment and he missed it... his response was villager if you need it that bad, I could help you out I'm not just a bartender you know (she answered: right, it's not like that, can you just call him he said if I needed him I could reach him here.) Antonio was still in bed when his phone rang, he answers; speak. Yo Antonio you got a visitor here man (What are you talking about?) Cocoa butter skin excellent condition real model type man, yo she hot! (You got me man) Hold on she's right here (handing her the phone)

Good morning, Rock?

In his confusion he asked: who is this?

Kareemah...

Yeah...Kareemah I never caught your name last night (setting up in bed) what time is it?

Its 10:30 I'm sorry for calling so early, it's just that I've been thinking about you since last night. Can I come over?

Sure, why not.

When Kareemah arrived, she could hear music by Prince playing insatiable in the distance as she approached to knock on

17

the door. As he opens the door her eyes did a quick review of his floor plain before she even took off her coat.

Wow you have a lovely place, I see you playing some Prince too.

Yeah, Prince is the man with the plain and controls my moves to get the job done.

Checking him up and down in all of the obvious places, yeah sure can move. I'm in love with him you know, we women find him extraordinary.

Absolutely, so you needed to see me huh and now I have a question for you.

Yes… she looked at him in his white T and black sweets. His eyes met hers…

What?

Her eyes spotted his island and that he was preparing something. You cook too that is so sexy walking into the kitchen.

A man has got to eat you hungry?

She walked slowly towards him as the song changed. She unbuttoned the coat sliding it down to meet the floor. She was beautiful in a soft gray and pink Casmir half shirt and short silk skirt that played upon her inviting thighs. Setting her upon the island in the kitchen, her body was designed two respond two his energy. His mouth opened to meet her sweetness giving into bated breath he surrenders as his hands explored and caress her body, leaving his inhibitions behind finding her desire to mold him. Slipping his index finger as ooh's and yes became repetitious sliding back and forth in continuous pleasure. He made her want to holler scream and shout as he fingers did the walking in and all about, she replied oh how you get your fingers to do that? Putting her leg on the chair, she liked it. (This is where they begin) Kareemah couldn't contain her emotions, gripping onto Antonio as he gets it good and wet, he submerges inside of her creamy cove. Ooh yes you feel so good... ooh ma... yeah baby... damn girl, sighs and heavy breathing set the mood.

Kareemah is floating on anything but air as her response is I love your technique.

No shit, but we can't happen like this.

Why I want to be with you?

I got too much going on right now.

Like what, I didn't come here to hear you say something like this!

My job for one and college takes up the rest, and he stopped... I'm not ready for a relationship.

Antonio, I feel you all inside me, you wake up my whole being. That night I saw you, you took my breath away don't tell me you didn't feel that.

Look let's just take this slow, I got too much on my plate; don't try to get inside my head! Ok, one day at a time.

I can work with that Rock. So what kinds of things do you like to do, I see you like art.

Not too much far from work and school all I have left is basketball.

ELIZABETH PERKINS

I like going to parities hanging out with my friends and talking on the phone.

Great just like a woman...

What was that?

Are you hungry I was fixing a little something before work?

Later that night Club Quest its packed and the women are lined up to get in some with reservations others paying at the door. Antonio is in the dressing room when Christopher walks in; have you ever had that good sex that instantly knocked you right out? Wow

Yep, slept like a baby too!

Men....its's in her mind, not what's in her pants, its what's in his heart...not what's in his pocket. People confused these days. Sex and money isn't everything. Neither one of those can keep a real soulmate...but most definitely will bring a lot of lying, cheating, mistreating and heartless people in your world.

Got that bit-ties number on speed dial!

Yo that's rude man?

Naw I'm being honest! Men who don't have shit going on in the bedroom need to be told just that. They want their egos stroked and their stroke game isn't up to par.

Right: Tyler chimes in; I was so knocked out shehad to shake me to wake me up (laughing) wow I got to call her...I'm about to do that now, laughing...

TEARS OF A BROKEN HEART

Louis comments: Now that's what I'm talking about!! I had a few little honeys come real damn close, but it takes a lot to knock this me out!! Yo that chick had some sex drive!

Yeah, right whatever; you know you like to go to sleep (laughing)

Come on now homie you know damn well only way a nigga can put Mandingo to sleep is possibly if she bought 2 or 3 of her friends to help him out!!

Antonio laughed so hard

Yo Ant Jimmy told me about this little honey that came in for you, you sharing?

Jimmy is always running his damn mouth...truth is that isn't nothing real today. Just fake fraud ass people. It isn't worth it anymore. Life without love is Death.

Oh yeah, so you hitting that or what? I know you had her hollering oh my god, thank you Jesus hallelujerrrrrr!

Nigh man she's just a fan you crazy, but that's a good one, walking out of the dressing room to do his set. I'm on and the ladies are calling for the booty man, you feel me man patting Louis on the back...

Ooh sounds like a gag order is in effect.

Order of protection against you!!!!!

I know right! They laugh so hard...

You going to hurt somebody!!!

Yeah well, I'll do what I can...

21

ELIZABETH PERKINS

The men continue talking meanwhile Antonio was oiling up his physique for his show, he can hear the women cheering in frenzy for more. The MC is queueing up the music, Chico DeBarge Physical Train. Antonio pop-locks his way slowly embodying the energy that is in the air. Rotating his hip and slowly lowering himself to the floor, he attempts to work the illusion of exotic sex and leaving a lasting impression on the minds of on looking women. As the music fades for the next dancer, he makes his way into the audience to collect on the giving hands of adoring women that offer not only money but sex and more. After his show he sets off into the dressing room to get dressed and out the back door of the club. He hears Kareemah's voice saying; you, okay?

What, what are you doing here I didn't see you in inside? Rain begins to come down and lighting streaks crosses the sky.

I didn't come in because I was being polite.

Like your approach.

You still didn't answer my question, are you okay?

Yeah, I just have a headache from this damn job. It's frustrating I just need a minute.

Come on let me take you home.

No, I'm done here soon, and I need the money.

Then I'll come over later.

No not tonight I just want to be alone.

SUNDAY

Sunday all is silent Antonio is playing Play Station enjoying the calm when a knock comes across the door. It's Kareemah; How bout lunch?

Sounds like an outing. They find themselves in a restaurant with a live jazz band. Antonio shares his plains with Kareemah about school and the opportunity's that he has set for himself. There is so much magic in the air between the two of them and after lunch he opens up his world to her. Giving Kareemah a tour of the University and visiting the Historic Buildings around the city. And as the evening comes to a close Antonio takes Kareemah home.

Thank you I had a nice time today.

Yeah, I did too. Kareemah is falling in love with Antonio that she begins to speak; I want to tell you something…

Please don't say it, remember we're taking it slow.

Yes, we are; you still hungry? She takes his hand and they go inside closing the door, they kiss their way into the bedroom. Kissing and getting him all aroused, kissing on his neck rubbing on his paints she could feel him getting erect. Pulling off their clothes she slides down further so anxious to touch him, whispering (can I taste it?) Her mouth was getting wet as he braced himself for the warmth of her mouth. Starting off slow, then deeper and deep she goes. Kissing him so sensual thinking (he tastes to go to her) Her hands stroked up and down as she licked sucked and stroked him into moaning pleasures, she loved the sounds he made from all the pleasure she was giving him.

ELIZABETH PERKINS

She knew he liked it as Antonio said: wait not yet. Lying her down on the bad moving his hands slowly up her thighs tasting her honey as she moans in sweet pleasure (ooh baby) making her quiver while in the moment. Reaching up with one hand he played and caressed her Brest while he teased and licked her preparing to make love to her. Antonio rose up and submerged deep inside of her cove, exploring all the passion and their energy became one. Kareemah hips responded in rapid motions (I want you baby please don't stop) the interlude was exciting Antonio was swept up in the scent of her body.

She was everything he wanted in a woman and more, making love to her this was everything the imagination could indoor it was nasty outrageous hot and raw mixed with that kind of hard pounding sex aroused his appetite for Kareemah. She was so good sexual stimulation of her walls had him wanting more despite his desire his juices free deep in her passion. And as they lay wrapped in each other's arms drifting off to sleep it began to rain and the winds whipped so hard the windows themselves shook as if the winds wanted in like strange sprits was trying to get in and Kareemah whispers softly; I won't ever hurt you…Antonio thought to himself; this is the real reason why Adam never left Eve? And he closed his eyes…

MONDAY

Kareemah woke up cold Monday morning reaching out for the warmth of Antonio's his body only to discover he was gone. She called out for him but no answer as she got out of bed to look for him, she looked around only to find a note taped to the front door reading (thank you Mss I had a really nice time, call me we'll get together sometimes or whenever I get some free time. Rock)

Kareemah was confused disappointed and disgusted in his note, she felt so sick this can't be happening like this I love him! She quickly called him, but his voice mail picked up. This is Antonio I since something is on your mind. Let's get it because you're running out of time BEEP!

Antonio I'm sorry if I pushed too hard you were right we should take it slow, I don't know what happened everything felt so right I don't know what to say. Hopefully, you'll let me into your heart; I mean you no harm I just want to love you with all that I am. Please call me when you get message. I promise I won't question your reasoning let's just start over Antonio please…

Antonio looks and listens to her message as she speaks, then puts on his headphones to set out for a long jog in the park.

Meanwhile Kareemah has gathered her girlfriends together crying her eyes out; I don't know what to say about him, but he's the first person I fell in love with, I've been celibate for a year. I thought he was going to be the one till this happened: I'm guessing he really doesn't know how much I love him.

I told him last night that I would never hurt him and before I first realized it, he was gone. He said he had a really nice time;

call me we'll get together sometimes whenever I get some free time. Rock I can't believe this, this is so wrong! I'm so upset and hurt by it. He chose to say he's done so basically; he chose what he's feeling over me. How could I have been so blind! Nothing in the world is going to make his actions justified-able. So, what was the point of leading me on? (Melissa holds her close) I'm so sorry babe! You're a good woman and these men aren't shit today. You must give them a dose of their own medicine girl, that's what I would do...

Why would anyone want to hide their feelings from people his job or whatever! that don't mean a thing, they are strippers too. I'm sure they have a life outside of dancing. Actions speak louder than words. The words he has said to me, he has never been in love with anyone if he ever fell in love before, I won't look for another relationship if we don't work out, and I'll do things just to try and make him happy.

But now, this one action of hiding hid feeling and leaving me a note! (Reading the note again) Thank you Miss I had a really nice time, call me we'll get together sometimes whenever we get some free time, Rock...I have fell in love with everything about him and how well we worked together as a team to get things done and picturing spending my life with him was what I wanted. Did I miss something along the way and he changed? How can he not understand how unappreciated I feel and that people who genuinely love each other would do anything to lift there partner up not push aside their feelings and act like what they did is ok. The cruelest thing you can do to a person is pretend that they mean more to you than they do.

I know exactly what you're going through Kareemah (Tonya digs into some Häagen-Dazs ice cream) it hurts because when you love someone you want to tell the world and want everyone to know, and for him to hide his feelings makes you think he can't possibly feel the same way you do (opening a bag of chips) been there done that.

TEARS OF A BROKEN HEART

Melissa: no feed that nigga his own shit so he knows how it feels. Then start ignoring him it works honey; men don't like to be ignored sometimes we have to do we have to do that. And if you see him on the street don't give him the time of day. If you see him first act like you talking to some old friend on the phone and keep it moving. Then watch his ass blow up your phone...

Clear chimes in: Damn girl you so fat! (Looking at Tonya laughing) you need prayer honey! And looking at all those food shows that's why your ass big now.

Tonya responds with: Shut up I only had two ribs one piece of chicken and one grilled cheese sandwich for lunch. But I had hibachi for lunch and I only had three plates, so get your life...

Okay greedy gut, but this is so honest and raw...I hate that you're going through this Kareemah, but we all have been there. Loving someone's son who doesn't deserve us.... life is hard... Love should not be like this...but men like that who have been hurt over and over tend to be very afraid of falling in love. So, don't be afraid or too stubborn to go the extra mile to show him you want him.

Sorry you're going thru this but I can see where he's coming from...not to defend him one bit but if it's who I think it is then I agree...he wants to be successful and that's fine, but you do need to keep in mind hearsay from other people can ruin a relationship just as well as a career. I don't think He did it to hurt you, but maybe more so to protect you and "y'alls" relationship.

I would think about why he did it from every view point. Is he a private person to begin with? It might not you he's hiding but his real self, they say half of men over 50 have erectile dysfunction and 35% of younger men do too because of their meat diet and other circumcision. Woman can have intercourse (sex) all day and be a little sore. But men are scared to admit they are sexually weak compared to a woman. So, they play the pimp role or the "Mack daddy" role to cover up their weakness. I would consider everything before you just let it go like that.

Wow that's crazy I don't know what's wrong with men seems to me they use women for their own gain. And why do most men want to have their cake and eat it too? Can anyone please answer that...?

Woo-cha and you don't deserve to be put on the back burner. Girl put your freak-um dress and get out there because there are plenty more fish in the sea... get yourself a boy toy and use that don't ask don't tell shit...

You know what? I hate to say this, but we women are so fucking weak and scared to be without a man! I hear it all the time at work, girl why I don't have a man or why he doesn't want me? We don't make him choose us! I blame us women for not having higher standards and we give them their cake and feed it to them too!

Hold on now: God said be modest in everything you do! Drink the wine but don't get drunk! Men prey on weak woman! They don't step to strong sisters with that mentally! Be fruitful and multiply with your girlfriend and future wife, not be a hoe about in the street! But women can be the dirtiest hoes too with shit like a girl needs a personal dick in her bag it's like having a spare fucking tire when I get a flat. And then he got her saying; I'm good with that just don't fall in love...He'll be your boy toy...

Some women just have low self esteem to even keep a man. They get all fat and let themselves go and expect a man to want their asses. You ever see a man you haven't seen in years say; damn girl you haven't changed, I've been in love with you forever. I'm still in love with you, and you start smiling all fucking stupid, then the next thing you know he got your cookies and gone! A woman should be humble and pass that nigga up because if he really loved you, y'all would still be together. You would be his back bone his strength his desire! Not his mother fucking stepping stool…A dog is a dog!!! Trust a man that's married or in a relationship will have no problem with getting naked or a room as long as you (being the operative word here) are set something up and keeping it between y'all knowing he got has women. And he will surely dick you down is really good as long as it stays between you only…Women are stupid too…it only takes one time to lie down and come up with a disease… when you lay down with dogs you get up flees (laughing).

Well, I don't see a problem with having your cake and eating it too. But people these days become homicidal when they find out you're biting off of multiple slices of different cake. I'm still riding with my man; he can eat and be marry all up and through my cake. Shit I'll even bake it if he's buying the ingredients; you know the bakeware, the china to serve it on and the silver to feed him with. People make life difficult by forgetting reciprocity. Give a little, so you both have a whole lot. In this case, buy the strawberries and sugar. Slice up the strawberries and pour the sugar over them, allow them to marinate overnight. The next evening have him grab the bowl while you lie across the bed and allow him to eat until he's full and you'resatisfied. Although I'm sure you should already know that…

You know too much of anything can hurt you! Cake, Drugs, liquor, Women! Just to name a few! Beside if u can have cow without buying the milk wouldn't you still drink it? Same concepts…. men only do what women allow them to…

I see guys I know that have good women at home all hugged up with other girls at my job and their girl or wife don't know about it… its crazy for me because I got to watch them and these other girls be all up in their faces like there the one…the trip part is they go home and play the innocent…and they think that shit is cool, that's why we women have to play inch-high private eye, going though their pockets and phone and shit.

Hold on now if a devoted man is taking care of his woman, not just sexually or financially, but spiritually and morally are you folks saying that the woman is a fool for baking herman's cake and feeding it to him? Showing him that she appreciates him and is willing to accept being his queen? Not every man has proven his worth, but don't get bogged down in that "some men aren't shit and all women are bitches" mentality. My man has his selfish ways and when he has his moments, I point it out, fall back and let him get it together. Just like he calls me spoiled. But together, he gives me what I need and desire and vice versa…

Just remember true love will always have ups and downs and there is nothing better than being in love. You have to decide if one bad fault is worth letting everything else go. When you decide to get married, I think that means that you have decided that from that time on you will work through anything and everything to be together. I hope which ever path you take it will end in total happiness. By the way my boyfriend is 10 years older than me and he found it hard to be completely public about our relationship for the first year of our relationship, because people do talk. And as silly as it is that's how he felt. Just an outside looking in opinion though.

Girl you better tell your brother to open up a can of whoop that ass if a brother isn't treating you right! Fuck all that, I had to tell a brother about himself and trust me next, he came to the bedroom with everything on point! It's come correct or don't cum at all (laughing). The girls stay on the mail bashing conversation all night…

TEARS OF A BROKEN HEART

Girl I was in this relationship with a man, remember Pettis? He didn't sleep with me he didn't spend time with me we didn't go nowhere together or do nothing together. He showed me no comfort and he had no sex game at all. He never told me I look good, beautiful or even noticed me. I feel so alone with him pulse we didn't even talk. I need all that in a man; I'm a woman that needs to feel loved and Pettis didn't make me feel that way. I told him that I needed him and wanted him, but he just wasn't there for me, I heard men telling me I look good talking to me and everything, but I need that from Pettis and he didn't give me that. I have tried and tried with him, but he just didn't get it. I really didn't need a man like that in my life. It's was time for me to make strong changes in the man for me, I didn't want to be in relationship with a man that is married and wont and yes Pettis was married.

And I started going out with other friends, well men. Because Pettis wasn't giving me what I needed. I went to an all-white party here a few years ago. And it seemed like a very mature and professional crowd. You know Business men and women, a few regular people here and there. Well, when I went to the bathroom, I didn't see two guys following me over there. As I got to the door, they pushed me in. One guy stood against the door while the other raped me, and when he was finished, the guy by the door took his turn.

They told me that if I told the police, they would kill me since they looked at my driver's license and knew my address. So, I got myself together and left out the back door. I have not been to a party, gathering or club since. Your guy sounds very protective of you from what I heard from what you told me. I still don't really deal with men. After my incident, I was so afraid of being naked with a man that I pushed quite a few away. But they are still friends with me to this day. It only took once for me before I stopped trusting any man that I did not know. Or one that offered me riches and crap. I have seen what the rich do. Whatever they want, and buy your silence or buy their way out of jail.

I know all too well about betrayal and being so heartbroken it disintegrates and blows away like the wind. Tears that soak the pillow so bad that you can't even sleep on it, I know all too well. I will guard my man's heart as if it was in my own chest, the only way he could break it is if he cut it out of me and I know he wouldn't do that because that would hurt him, and he wouldn't do that to me. I was married once to a paralegal, but he fell in love with the money and drugs I filed for divorce after 10 years of marriage because I couldn't beat the coke. But I loved being married and that broke my heart. I guess I got married too young...

We all know that the root of evil is the love of money. I do like the things you can get with money... Like a house, and vacations and gifts.... And since my sister robbed me blind when we shared a place together, I'm a little more focused on trying to save my money back up. But that won't stop me from doing things for myself or my man. And I don't even associate with people that do drugs. I saw what drugs can do to people by watching my sister as she went down the drain.

You want to hear the craziest thing a man told me? To stop wearing underwear to allow the angel of the air to freshen my sacred flower further and become "positively celibate" by not allowing intercourse until Ihave had as much oral sex as I wanted. And I would notice having up to 30 multiple orgasms. Just encourage my mate to use his tongue and explore my sacred flower and do not be "shy" let him know what I like and what I want. If it feels good explore it further. There is no place I should not let him explore with his tongue including my anus. Because the womb orgasms are rare but easy for women to achieve because analogues most women adore. But who wants to give analogues to a woman eating animal flesh?

TEARS OF A BROKEN HEART

Who wants to give cunnilingus (head) when a woman's sacred flower (Vagina) smells like dead fish because of the trim ethyl amines from decomposed animal flesh? So do me a favor and stop wearing panties, stop eating anything that has eyes and is not grown from the soil and bless as many men as deserve it with a view of your incredible beauty including wearing mid-thigh dresses and just bending over, going up stairs, etc. and allow men to see your sacred flower without any fanfare or money exchanges. The girls laughed so hard that night and the day was forgotten.

TUESDAY

That following Tuesday Antonio is in the shower when his ringing and at first, he couldn't hear it, but then he heard his voicemail chime in; this is Antonio I since something is on your mind. Let's get it because you're running out of time BEEP! Antonio, I know you got my message yesterday, why haven't you called me back? Please don't keep me hanging, if you want nothing to do with me just tell me…

Antonio turned off the water grabbing a towel and walked into the living room, pushing the button to receive the call as he walked into his bed room to get dressed and go to the University. Where he was working on his master's degree in criminal law, he put in all the time he could because he was determined to pass the bar with flying coolers. He reads over the material and is soon engulfed in his work.

CRIMINAL LAW & PROCEDURE

Crime is a huge subject – it's essentially two subjects combined into one. Because each of the six MBE subjects receives almost equal coverage, not everything in Crime will be tested. In other words, it's a hard subject to predict because inevitably something you would expect to be tested won't come up. With that said, you'll see a lot of the common law crimes. But coverage of criminal procedure principles is sporadic. You may see just one or two questions on a topic as big as 4th Amendment search and seizure. A couple of small things to watch for on the bar exam, but particularly the MBE.

DOUBLE JEOPARDY

Double jeopardy sometimes appears as an answer choice, but it can't be easily dismissed as a red herring. Make sure you review double jeopardy *see (Criminal Law & Procedure – cards 61 & 62)* and don't be surprised if it comes up as the subject of a question – not just as an answer choice – one or two times.

TEARS OF A BROKEN HEART

BEEP! Hey, I have been struggling all day about what to do about us; the answer is I'm not going to give up because I love you, despite the differences that we have had I miss you greatly. I'm quite strong and can respect what you want. You don't have to worry about that, I wish we could erase all the bad parts of the last two days I love and respect you infinitely.

WEDNESDAY

Wednesday Antonio leaves early for the library when he hears his phone ringing. He listens before walking out the door. This is Antonio I since something is on your mind. Let's get it because you're running out of time BEEP! Antonio! Now I know you check your messages... why are you being so mean to me! Why are you messing with my head like this? Can you please tell me what I have done for you to have stopped all communications with me? In my last message is said...BEEP! She calls back getting the voice mail; this is Antonio I since something is on your mind. Let's get it because you're running out of time BEEP! It's not my intent to bother you; I'm not asking anything, please at this point. I don't know where we stand with each other. I hope that we are still friends. I'm confused one minute you treat me with such loving care than hurt me the next why?

BURDENS OF PROOF AND BURDEN-SHIFTING STATUTES

We've noticed several questions that involve burden of proof issues. These questions may ask about the burden of proof required for asserting a defense, the burden required for conviction, or whether a statute that changes a burden is constitutional. Know the burden requirements for these scenarios.

Meanwhile Kareema was at home opening a strange chest and carefully removing a bundled scarf wrapped in it was some oils and some candles. She was preparing for a bonding, knowing it wasn't the right time to be casting spells she remembers (when you put out energy you get energy back, not knot knowing if its good or bad) but she continued anyway.

As part of the preparation for casting a spell, rub a candle with anointing oil while concentrating on the purpose of the spell. The formula of the oil will be determined by the purpose of the spell. Or, write a spell on a candle and then burn it. Inside the scarf were a candle that represented a man and a candle that represented a woman. She was about to perform a love spell the New Moon was the best time being that was the time for new beginnings. She also knew that after a terrible year filled with a lot of unhappiness and a very disastrous relationship

She waited for a quiet time then she anointed both candle all the while intoning her love interest; what she hoped for i relationship. She asked to be coupled with someone kind generous and who would be faithful to her. She asked someone who was ready and willing to accept her love. She asked that he be the one person in the universe with who was meant to be, and vice versa. His character was the most important thing to her, along with the ability to be open to her love. Then lit the candles and said the love spell over them. The essence of the spell was a request for the Universe to recognize her need for love, her declaration that she was as entitled to it as everyone else in the Universe. She added a request that the right person be brought to her, stating where he was in this universe.

While the candles burned, she thought about to all the times she had let good men go because she was unable to meet the needs of the men she was involved with. She thought about all the times she allowed her desperate need for closeness to someone, anyone, lead her into a destructive and abusive relationships. She watched as the candles burned, and the woman's candle burned the quickest. She saw that when it burns that it was crying and her soul was crying along with it for all the missed opportunities she had in life. And for all the sorrow and abusiveness she allowed herself to experience. She watched as the candle shed purple tears and finally burn down.

As the candle that carried her name burned down and finally went out and she knew she had cleared the baggage of the past from my inner aura, and made herself ready to accept a new relationship into her being. She knew that to initiate a new relationship while still holding on to the past and past energies is self-defeating. It took a while, but she didn't forget her new vow to open herself up to the good energy around her. Unbeknownst to her she opened a portal to allow demons to come within her being to use her as a vessel of negativity and spirits would possess her.

That night Kareemah called Antonio knowing she would get his answering machine. This is Antonio I since something is on your mind. Let's get it because you're running out of time

THURSDAY

Thursday, he works on his body set-ups, push-ups and lifting all to create the grand-design for the women's minds while he's entertaining them. When again his phone rings? This is Antonio I since something is on your mind. Let's get it because you're running out of time BEEP! Hearing Kareemah's voice… I have a terrible headache this morning and can't see straight. I got up early on my way to work, going to stop for a cappuccino. Listen can we patch up things between us? Please call me…I respect what you're doing, and I want to be a help for you with your success in life, love you baby…

He then set out for his morning jog before work… while jogging he thinks I can't believe her persistence in constantly calling me, don't she get it already, she is either a crazy stalker or she really cares. I can't let this girl get to me like that, and I can't believe I'm really thinking about her, it must be the sun because I'm tripping….

Later that night at Club Ever-Quest lights were down low, music changed to R. Kelly's Tempo Slow, Antonio crawls to the floor and over to bottles of wine in the middle of the stage. Taking an imaginary bath as his glossy body slid over to one lucky woman, licking around the top of the bottle. With his tongue slowly, his tongue slid up and down around and back up to the top before sliding it inside of the bottle, pulling it out slowly and offering her a drink.

She goes to take a sip and pours it on herself totally missing her mouth completely do to being in a trance of his offer. She was hypnotized by the things he did with his mouth. The women went wild over him; he was the most sensational dancer at the Quest. Later on, back in the dressing room a note was waiting for him on the table.

ELIZABETH PERKINS

Antonio reads; I'm sitting here writing my heart out to you, to show and prove my love to you, because I don't want to lose you... please call I'm scared too, you took me to another level as well. Please call me...

That evening at the Quest the men was talking trash about the honey women that just entered the club. Look man I just told the freak my ass is sweating that means it's wet and she can lick it, I'll even spared them cheeks for her!

Antonio laughing: Man, you sick...

Man, I gave her that ripe banana... Yeah!

Women today are crazy as hell. They complain about love and men when they don't want it. A good man can't even get a good woman. Most of them are taken and the rest are not good. I'm starting to see no point in being good to women. Fuck it...

Charles interrupted: Yo man you always reading, what you got there?

Antonio: just studying... hey, you remember that women that called for me last week?

Saturday... Yeah hot little honey... what about her?

She wants me to be her man... but... I'm not trying to be with her like that...

Why not? I got this fine ass women cross town that loves what I do for her. I am not gone lie she got me, she be bending over picking up shit around the house (you know doing regular shit) and I be peeping at her from the rear, man what a rump roast. I get up on herand start licking her from behind and massage those buttocks, man she wifey material!

TEARS OF A BROKEN HEART

Yeah, she fine but I'm not ready for a serious relationship…

What do you mean? Yo Ant you been drinking because this philosophical side of you is creepy man (laughing)

Naw man, seriously she's too good for me.

Get the fuck outta here! A hoe is a hoe…

Why women got to be a hoe with you man? She's a good girl…

I'm not saying all women are hoes, just the ones I fuck with no names like Monday, Tuesday, Wednesday, Thursday, Friday, Saturdays and Sundays are mutable (laughing) it is what it is, you now? Where did you meet this, good girl?

I met, well… we met here.

Aww shit! Come on man? You know how many betties come in here on the regular?

I know… but she's better than any of the women that have been coming in here.

If she's all that, why don't you ask her out?

I don't have time right now… pulse I can't give her what she wants…

Depending on what she wants, just let her know you got shit to do, keep it real. If you want her and it's meant to be than man, go for it man.

Yeah, I hear you…

ELIZABETH PERKINS

She got kids?

Naw she straight…

If she's the one, go for it like I said I got me a little honey and cross town and she sweet as hell.

Then, why are you digging these women out behind the flirt room?

I'm just cashing in man… like the pastor said the pot is kind of short (they laugh) got to dig a little deeper…

Man, you're sick…

Sick but true and let the church say amen…

Amen…

FRIDAY

That Friday Kareemh is writing her last letter to the love of her life, implementing a spell that when opened it would never close again: Antonio have you ever wanted something or someone so bad it hurts, leaving you breathless. I miss you so much and I can't sleep at night thinking about you. I go through the week without you by my side, these feelings I can't hide inside. I wanted you to take your time and open up to me. I wanted to know everything about you. Your likes, dislikes... your favorite food, movie and song... I wanted to know what melts your heart, what makes you happy. I wanted to know how passionate of a man you are. Tell me what pleases you sexually, emotionally and physically...You make me feel so alive, I need you like I need to breath and I can't see going on living in the same city with you knowing we will never be... she got in her car and drove over to Antonio loft. Parking her car, she gently kissed the letter and got out to put it in his mailbox and walked away.

Antonio opened the door to see her walking away, he immediately said: you didn't call me today…

Turning around Kareemah said: should I have?

Why me?

What?

Why do you want to be with me?

Is this a trick question?

No…I have told a few people that I trust about this woman that has me captivated... as well as my fear of not being good enough for you. I told you, I am so much into you that I am not sure if I will live up to your expectations. I'm not the perfect looking or acting guy at times... and I am so used to not being important to a woman unless I was spending money or doing something for her. So, yes, I am a little afraid. But all I can do is wait and hope for the best. I know how much I can love a woman, but I have never truly known love from a woman... why me?

Because I am unlike no woman you have ever met. I'm the best of all because I was raised by my father and I know how to love a man. I go after his heart in having your heart insures me that I have you all to myself and you will be mine.

I can't spoil you, but I would love to be yours; I just hope I am worth it. Either way, I will do my best to show you who I am, and how I like to make you smile. You will see very soon. My affection for you is growing and I have yet to even smell your hair. You have some power princess... I am in love with you as I know you right now. So, I know that once I get to hold you, my heart will be yours and yours alone...

You make me feel so good baby and I love you as well.

Do you up princess?

Yes, I am.

Ever-Quest is off laments to you, I don't need every dude that works there knowing my women, and even if you think I trust them. You never know what might make a man snap and do something stupid. Just trying to look out for you princess... Plus, I don't like every guy hanging around me and my women. When we are together...I want it to be me and you... Not me you and other guys, especially other entertainers. Part of my job as your potential man is your safety, your happiness, your love and your rock. So, I will do what I can to be that for you no matter what…as long as you allow me to.

Kareemah walks over to him and takes her letter out of his mailbox, putting it into her bag, her eyes showing so much sadness… thank you so much I can see you will keep me spoiled with your words of encouragement. It's rare to find a man that speaks the way you do, seems Prince has a rival in words to my heart. All I can say is thank you for being who you baby never change that about you because this man has captured my heart. I'm the one that is very much afraid of love, like a dear taking a cool drink at the spring. Then only to hear the sound of movement she runs. But I like your approach, so I stay to see more.

You're still so ever beautiful, kissing her lips softly… And trust me princess, I'm a one-man woman… and hopefully my woman is as affectionate as I am… As far as pleasing my woman goes… There is nothing I would not do to give that satisfaction to you. Every inch of your body, would be for my tasting, kissing and touching. I do require lots of passion and heat in the bedroom though. Without passion, it's just doing the "F" word, and that gets boring…Antonio puts on some jazz music… Umm, are you thirsty, would like something to drink?

Thank you, baby, I agree with you Antonio I love making love to my man every time I'm with you. There should be no place on the body I cannot kiss, lick, suck, or anything else. And I love to hear my man whisper sweet things to me in the process. That's a turn on…

Antonio takes a sip of his juice: ok, you are about to make me go there... but I got to get in this hot water before you cause me to forget myself (Laughing to himself) But, really can I have my letter back now?

Oh, it's nothing.

ELIZABETH PERKINS

If it's nothing than why is it in your bag?

Because its mine...

Really, then why did you take it out of my mailbox? Holding out his hand; give it here I won't read it... she hands it to him and he snatches it, opening it he begins to read it saying: You have left an indelible mark on my heart, tears of joy rush from my eyes like a fountain when I think about you being in my corner like you have been.

When I got your last massage after all that insanity, my happiness meter went off the chart, because I couldn't have thought that you really cared. At the base of everything else we are for each other, thank you for being my friend. Never forget that what we are is bound by all the secrets of a black velvet pouch and cannot be dissolved by anyone but us...I will yet honor and live by it until I close my eyes in eternal slumber... Antonio finishes reading the letter to himself. He lifts his eyes to meet hers as she says: I promise I won't go anywhere...

Kareemah walked over to him she says: I have an opportunity to live a dream shared by many of your fans, and it's monumental butI need one more thing Antonio?

Anything, just name it?

I need your heart...Kareemah starts kissing Antonio with anticipation of wanting more.

Hold on now princess I'm about to head out to work... Relax and make yourself comfortable I have to finish my workout. He goes back to his sit-ups, push-ups and lifting...Kareemah studies his body from head to toe. He was fine with all that strength and all that sweet dripping all over his body. Just looking at him ignited a fire deep inside her. She was going to make sure she never loses him again. Her mind was racing as she heard the winds picking outside hitting at the windows with force…

That night at Quest things got hot, women was drinking and partying hard, and most of them were real fucked up. The women were loud and snapping: Shake that shit baby!

Through it and I'll catch it!

That's a fine motherfucker right there!

Ooh look at how he pops' that thing.

I bet he can work that ass, whoever got him I know she is fucking the hell out of him.

He can break me off some of that!

Oh shit! Yeah baby…

Meanwhile in the dressing room Crag and Victor are working over two women thoroughly.

Crag: yeah baby…sucks that shit. Ooh yeah just like that, eat that dick ma… damn girl, ahh shit! Sass… yes, work that…Victor is behind her pumping away: just don't stop grinding that ass girl. Antonio walks in on them; shaking his head he just grabs his things and leaves.

SATURDAY

Saturday morning Antonio wakes up to a knock at his door. Aww damn don't people sleep around here now a day. Yo... the knocking continues... what the? He opens the door. Kareemah is waiting at the door: I missed your show last night... can I get a private dance?

Don't you sleep?

I slept last night, I'm up now. How did your night go?

Crazy... women are wilder than men.

What do you mean?

Forget it... come in make your-self comfortable, I'm a get a shower and wake up. He goes into the bathroom to start his shower. Oh yeah please whatever you do don't mess with my paperwork on my desk. He goes into the bathroom and gets into the shower. Kareemah could hear the shower water running as she moves towards the bathroom. The song speechless playing in her head by Beyoncé, heat stemmed up the hall as she moved closer to the door. It was slightly opened, and she slowly pushed it open a little more. She stud there in her silence watching him, her hand slid across her stomach. Her body became aware of her touch, deep inside of her cove in response it began to throb. As her hands lowered to meet her warm cove, she began to gently message with the possibility of him inside of her. She closed her eyes slowly putting her head back; taking a breath, she opened her mouth. Sensing she was there, Antonio stepped out of the shower, his body was dripping wet... kneeling in front of her, just watching her he leaned in closer.

TEARS OF A BROKEN HEART

She could feel the heat of his breath upon her. She looked down at him than the warmth of his mouth embraced her. Kissing and licking her slowly as in an intimate kiss, his plump lips devouring the sweetness of her juices. As her passions releases Antonio rises up telling her to assume the position? Pressing her up against the cool bathroom tiles, he delivers extensive tantalizing blows of extreme pleasure. Kareemah could feel his breath on her neck heightening her arouses... she enjoyed the way he worked her body, her porcelain olive legs parted more to receive his bronze shaft. He long stroked nice and slow until he exploded inside of her. His body twitched in pleasure, kissing her back... now let me finish my shower, I got to get to the library before it closes... he kisses her face, okay?

Can I go with you?

No, why don't you get up with me later before I go to work.

Umm...ok, I have to stop by my girlfriends anyway. Umm, can I use your phone?

Yeah... you don't have to ask, lock up before you go.

Kareemah uses the phone to call Alisha; where's this girl at? The phone just rings (sighs) she hangs up... she can hear Antonio singing in the shower and she thought about telling him she was leaving but no, she just walked out locking the door behind her.

Kareema was driving home when she noticed a strange light in the sky Kareema thought it was an Airplanes flying overhead. Then another light appeared and intertwined with the other light she thought was a star. The sky light up with lighting, she thought it was going to rain furiously. The air pressure temperature and moisture changes, differences between one place and another, the light hovered overhead.

ELIZABETH PERKINS

The atmosphere was changing to a degree that it is hot, cold, wet, dry, calm, stormy than clear and cloudy the light was so bright that she put both hands in front of her to get a better glimpse. And as she was peering through her fingers, she saw another pair of hands merging with her own hands and disappeared into hers. Somewhere within her being she heard the mere utterance of a phrase "You shall wait until I return" the cursed forced to wander the earth and being unable to die until the Second Coming. The average atmospheric conditions changed, her head began spinning and she was having vague memories of travel and journeying to an orbit around Earth, what appear to be other planets.

The abductors displayed harsh physical forced medical examinations on her body. She awoke outside of her home no longer in her ca, she realizes she was in a different location and thought it was strange experiencing the missing time she checked the time: Whoooaaaaaahhh! I must be having some kind of déjà vu; I could have sworn I was driving. She gets into her car and heads home…

When she arrived home, she spots her Alisha car, she parks and gets out. Walking towards the house Alisha turns around, Hey, Miss. Where have you been, I've been worried sick about you.

I'm fine I spent the night over a friend's house.

Yeah right, what friend?

Come in I'll tell you all about it, the women go inside and Kareemah is so excited she is talking up a storm about her and Antonio. I'm good and I'm in love!

With Alisha being much older, her response was: Whatever happened to I had a good day at work and just home? But I do have one question if I am not being too noisy, how did you and this Antonio end up together?

I met him by chance one day, she lied. He brought a young teen into the community center that he found on the street crying. Turned out she ran away from home. So, since then he has been such a great person, calling to check on her and things.

Oh, wow he sounds like a great guy; he did a wonderful thing for the young teen I hope she is alright.

Yeah, she is but that wasn't the first time she had ran away and because of reoccurring events she was taken from her mother and placed in a home. He has been a pretty good friend and I was thinking about doing whatever I could to make him mine.

But alas, we shall only ever be friends. From what he tells me. But, we won't spend all our time talking about him. That would be weird but just know that I would never want to see him hurt. He has a very soft heart for a man in this day and age.

I see; were you going to keeping things under wraps until now. At least he told you already you must be a good friend.

Yeah, he is a good friend, butI need to know I will feel safe with him being I have a hard time trusting men. But from what I know of him I'm finding my heart wanting to be with him, you know. But I have no intention on hurting him at all Alisha, please keep this between us I'm not ready to tell him about that yet.

My mouth is closed. You have my word.

Thank you, Alisha, you're my favorite's friend.

You say so, now what are you guys' planning?

ELIZABETH PERKINS

Nothing we're just enjoying each other.

Nothing wrong with that I'm jealous, you found a great man, and he has a sexy ass delicious looking woman.

I'm excited about him Alisha and he does have a sexy quality to him, I'm just glad he is all mine.
Well, I am glad that you found a man like him. There are so many of us that would pass him by, for the other guys that keeps us wet from how they look or act. I was like that most of my youth, and went from pretty dog to pretty dog. And I think that's what made me become bisexual. I got tired of getting dogged by men, and when I wanted a decent one, they didn't want me because of the attitude I had developed. So, please treat him good. Be that woman that he needs and deserves.

I will Alisha I promise he is in good hands with me girl. And I understand how you feel I once had a woman in my life I was in love with but because of her career she moved away from me. I didn't tell Antonio that because I knew he wouldn't understand, how do you tell a man that? But I am so happy with him, you know it's funny I never thought I would meet my potential husband like this but you know I'm really feeling him and it feels so good.

You would be surprised to what men would understand these days. I'm not sure if you have realized it but he seems very wise and probably has seen a lot in his field. Besides, you may not believe it but I'll tell you something I don't think you guys have discussed. Dancers have pretty much dated nothing but bisexual women. But that's not hard considering that today, most women are bisexual. So, I am sure he would not have an issue with you being bisexual. Not many men do as long as you are not sleeping around with women behind their backs (laughing) I made a joke. But for real, if you do mess with women, never leave your man out if he is a good man. That's one way to run him off.

TEARS OF A BROKEN HEART

I feel you Alisha, I will tell him because he should know everything about me. And your joke was funny I'm still smiling, I'm glad we're friends I don't have too many friends because people are judgmental you know. And you are right men are a trip I seen men that tell me in not dark enough. And I struggle with my complexion all the time; it's a trip feeling like I don't fit in anywhere.

Struggle no more beautiful, it seems like your guy has only one thing he is into and that's a woman that act like a woman. I think you have made a good impression on him.

I pray I'm enough for him, but I intend to keep him happy always.

Why do you feel you are not enough for him? That's the first thing you have to get over. Never doubt yourself because then you will start to doubt your man.

Yeah, I know, but he is so well renowned to the world and so travailed. I just want to make him happy and pray he is not color struck because to me a black woman is a black woman you feel me. He is a man that will knock me off my feet and I'm starting to feel him inside, you know. Antonio is everything I want in a man, usually men want me because of what I look like but not Antonio, he just wants me.

Men like to see what they do for a woman, and know that the woman likes it. I don't think he is color struck and your skin tone is beautiful girl. Most men would love to be in his shoes when he touches and kisses it, and I know he will because that dude is a freaky ass guy, come on girl he's a stripper!

I feel you on that (laughing) trust me I'm ready, but we're going to take it slow first (laughing).

That makes me warm inside seeing a couple blossoming.

ELIZABETH PERKINS

You're a beautiful friend Alisha no one understands a women's heart like you do.

Flirting with me, are you? I might have to come have a threesome if I'm not careful.

(Laughing) you are a mess girl I love it!

So, what are you dating this guy?

We are friends, but we gone work on that.

Aww no you didn't. You didn't give him your cookies, did you?

No (she lied)

Yes, you did, you lying ass!

Kareemah smiled slyly…

So, what he is fine, I want details…

Yeah, he is (hesitantly) he's also a stripper…

A stripper girl you know they be hitting everything that comes through them doors honey.

Antonio is not like that!

(Mimicking Kareemah) Antonio is not like that! Whatever.

You don't know him he's nice.

And you do? Whatever you going to Lena's party tonight?

Oh yeah, is Sebastian gone be there?

TEARS OF A BROKEN HEART

You know he is; she is twisted over that boy.

Where she at anyway?

She's home.

We should go over there, with her crazy ass.
Yeah, let's go…

Later that night at Ever-Quest the women were willing over dancers. Antonio was sitting in the dressing room thinking when Crag walks in shouting: Yowzah, Yowzah, Yowzah! What's popping up in here?

Nothing much…

I feel you dog, the money ain't jumping off tonight. All these broke ass women, not one private dance.

Yeah…

What's on your mind man cause you ain't hear shit I said, oh and I have a copy of that CD you wanted.

What?

Nevermind man, something's got you fixed and it isn't this damn job?

Naw man… I'm just tired.

Crag peeps outside the curtain… did you see the new guy? I hear he's from Philly… what's his name Toy, Troy or something messaging himself to get mojo working, popping his hips and slowly tearing away his pants exposing one leg at a time. Ticking and popping his way to center stage to do his set. Twirling and tugging at his pants pulling them away. Flipping into a full split rocking with it, worming up to make his mans jump up and down.

The women go wild over the things he can do with all that he has to work with. They start pushing to get a closer look, shoving and pulling on each other getting mad because one is on him more than the other. The women start throwing glasses and bottles than they start fighting. That party was craziest party ever seen, a real hot mess. Two fights broke out and this one woman was beating the other woman in the face with her fist. Antonio never seen a woman beat the snot out of a woman before, it was freighting. The bathroom pips busted all over the floor and some people was dancing in that mess, they didn't even care. The women fought in a drunken madness, when the lights come up, the party was over.

Antonio gets out through the back door and down the alley to his car. He could see the women coming out of the building. He gets in his car and makes a U-turn and takes the long way home, on his way the thinks about Kareemah. That girl is nothing but trouble I don't know why I bother, she pretty cute though…. Damn I'm hungry! He heads for the WAWA to get a Shorty and a soda before going home.

Once home he checks his messages (click) hey baby it's mom I was calling to see how you're doing with your classes. Your sisters are going to Hershey Park; they have extra tickets and wanted to know if you wanted to go? Anyway, call me later baby bye…

Hey, Antonio its Kareemah sorry I couldn't catch you before you went to work. Anyway, I was calling just to talk to you, later bye…

Antonio starts pulling off his clothing and makes a B-line for a shower to wash away the night he just had. And after his shower he slumps on the sofa to eat and watch some television, and was sleeping before the commercial commenced. He fell into a deep sleep waking up early the next morning, sat up and looked out the window. How beautiful the sunrise was, and how lucky he was to be able to witness it at its very beginning. The deep purple sky with its thin orange edge was just enough light for me to see my still sleeping honey brown angel with her tousled hair barely covering her lovely face. We had made passionate love the night before, and I could still hear her soft, purr-like moan in my ear and feel the sting left in my shoulders from her tiny nails, she looked so peaceful, but I could still see the remains of a devilish smirk on her lips.

    I thought about the sweet taste of her ambrosia generated by a ripping climax...hmmm, how very sweet it tasted. With that image in my head, I very carefully crawled under the covers and started kissing her inner thighs, moving closer and closer to her warm, wet slit. Maybe she was in a dream state, for I could feel her body move back and forth in perfect rhythm with my oral endearments. The more I kissed her inner lips, the wider her legs spread to receive my tongue, which by now was darting in and out in a hungry fashion. I heard her moan so sweetly, and then felt her hands on the back of my head, pressing it closer, and spreading her legs even wider. I clutched her thighs with both hands and pulled her steaming hole close, by now my tongue tickling her inner walls. She responded by moaning loudly and thrusting her hips to my eager mouth, her movements getting wilder and wilder, her moans becoming cries of passion, until finally exploding all over his face...he jumped up in bed, oh baby, what a way to wake up!!

SUNDAY

Sunday came in with the sunlight warming his face; the light bothered his sleep as he turns over for some shade. Sleeping lightly, he can hear the television program on saying something about Healthy Meals, so he turns his head to take a peep at it. Laying there for a minute he watches a little more before gradually setting up. Getting up he goes to the bathroom as he yawns and stretches his way to the toilet to pee. Then he turns on the water to brush his teeth and wash his face. Looking into the mirror he says: what do I got to do today? Walking into the bed room setting on the bed contemplating his day, he looks at the phone and picks up the receiver and starts dialing.

His sister answers: Hello?

Hey baby.

Hey Ant.

What you doing today?

I'm about to cut your sister if she doesn't turn back to my movie.

(Laughing) yeah, ya'll crazy…

Neal voce comes across the receiver asking questions: who you talking to?

Lacy says: nun of your-business… and the sibling rivalry starts with them.

Give me the phone hussy, your-man. Hello who dis?

TEARS OF A BROKEN HEART

Antonio shakes his head. Y'all are crazy.

I'm about to rock her (laughing) nah for real though, you coming over here Ant?

Yeah, in a little bit, mom said ya'll going to Hershey Park?

Yeah, Cristal got tickets on her job, we are rolling out Thursday morning.

How many tickets y'all got left?

Hold on, how many tickets we got left?

Why?

Because Ant wants to know, that's why?

He doesn't need to know all that…

Antonio responds with: what did she say? Tell her to shut up and just answer the question (laughing)

(Laughing) she so dumb… Psych-nah she got two left.

I want them.

Who you taken one of your lame-o girlfriends (laughing)

Nah she's just a friend, where's mom and dad?

They went to the store; you know how dad is. He can't just get to the store and get one thing, so they gone be a while.

You right…

When you coming over?

ELIZABETH PERKINS

Later (his other line is clicking) let he hit you back someone's calling me.

Alright I'll see you later…

Yeah… he switches calls… yeah?

It's Delilah on the other line… what you doing?

Chilling right now, where you at?

In town with my girl…I'm about to come over there after I drop her off.

Oh, I'm about to roll out.

Wait for me I want to go with you.

I'm striate I'll get up with you later.

Okay then call me when you get home.

Alright! They hang up and Antonio gets dressed and heads out the door, his first stop is something to eat, then O.V.G to see his sisters for a minute and pick up the tickets. He enjoyed visiting with family, they were his life, and nothing could break the bond that they had. Just give up the ticket's girl!

So what chicken-head you taken with you to need two tickets boy?

I don't chill with chicken heads girl, now give me the tickets! Here, and be on time because we aren't waiting on you.

Shut up girl, where mom at?

They didn't get back yet?

TEARS OF A BROKEN HEART

What they buying the whole store? Tell mom I'll call her later.

Okay, dang you leavin'?

Yeah, I got things to do; getting into his car his last stop was the shopping center because he was low on food. You know shopping is the most boring thing to do but I got to do it. Milk, eggs, butter, cheese, ground meat, chicken ground, turkey sandwich, meat, noodles, mayo, mustard, potatoes, onions, garlic, canned veggies, fresh veggies, lettuce tomatoes, whole chickens, chicken breast boneless skinless, pasta, spaghetti sauce, tomato pastes, tomato sauce, Alfredo sauce, jalapenos, lettuce, cucumbers, fresh tomatoes, cottage cheese, butter, and condiments.

Later that evening Antonio is at his computer online he hadn't noticed the time when a knock came across his door… he gets up to go answer the door; opening the door, standing before him was Kelly an old girlfriend from too long ago. She draping herself around him saying; it's still whipped cream in the evening, right? With a mischievous look in her eyes she asks, are we alone?

Antonio gently pushed her off of him saying; what are you doing here?

I was in town for a while, so I thought I'd just stop by, pushing her way into his home and placing the whipped cream on the coffee table. I missed you Rock…

Uh, to tell you the truth I was on my way out… umm… he went to grab his jacket while asking, how long are you here for…? Putting on his jacket he leads her to the door while quickly walking behind her.

Well, I just got here yesterday, and slow down damn!

ELIZABETH PERKINS

I've had a lot on my mind lately, things have busy for me you know.

Yeah but, she turned around massaging the front of his paints; did you miss me?

Hah… not really, he moves her hand away.

Your just being mean Rock, I got in last night and you were on my mind so tuff, I thought I'd come over and stay a while with you while I'm here.

Can't do that right now; look I'm not trying to be rude but I really have to go.

Why don't you think about it…please Rock?

Right, look I thought about it and I'm going to have to pass.

Why… you got a girlfriend or something? Trust me, I'm a big girl and we're friends…

I know, and I want to keep it that way, now I really do have to go Kelly. He gets into his car and before he could drive off Kelly walks over to his car window, as he lets the window down. Kelly says; same old Rock hidden behind those glasses, hiding them beautiful eyes. It's a shame though… you're too fine to keep holding back what you feel. He smiles at her saying; thank you that was sweet, it was good seeing you again Kael... Now if you don't mind, I really have to go, driving off…

As he takes a short drive he reminisces on his father's words; Messing with those girls out there can fuck your head up boy. He responds to his thoughts; I hear you pops; I hear you. He turns onto his block and parks the car. When he starts walking to the door the winds blow stronger and he hears (we…will…devour) the winds were whispering to him. He looks around but sees nothing; thinking to himself that's strange going inside. Once inside he decides to call Delilah: Hey princess, sorry it took me so long to call you back. I had to grab something to eat and didn't want to be eating in your ear on the phone. And I had to stop by the mall for a little shopping for tomorrows show, I have nothing wear for the show and that was driving me crazy. I really need to upgrade my closet (he laughs to himself) because the things I have in there are so obsolete now… what are you up to beautiful?

Went to church today and after that had dinner with a few of the church members. I had grilled chicken and red beans/rice. I would love to cook a nice dinner for you sometimes Antonio (she listens for his response) but right now I'm doing laundry and getting myself ready for next week. Other than that, I'll be writing in my special book, and sitting back and letting the sun go down on me.

Damn girl has a beautiful, sensuous spirit about you that comes across wonderfully! Not trying to be "Nosy" but just being the inquisitive man that I am. I sometimes ask a lot of questions! Like what are you writing about?

Just some of my thoughts mixed with poetry.

Poetry huh, read something to me.

Blushing, it's not ready yet.

So, read it anyway, I won't say a word, promise?

Okay (thinking I really shouldn't this is crazy) than she clears her thought getting ready and hoping he don't think she's nasty or perverted for her writings because men get the wrong idea quick about women and start talking dirty on the phone and phone sex because that's not what's it's about. Bearing your thoughts is like opening the book of your life to someone. She

ELIZABETH PERKINS

hesitantly begins to recite the words flowing from the pages of her mind.

JUST FOR YOU

I'm sitting in bed with a blue t-shirt on Indian style with nothing on underneath. And I can feel the heat of my body rising to meet my hands and I'm thinking of you. Thinking of the wonder of you penetrating me and I welcome the thought. Wanting to pull my toy from under my bed but that wouldn't satisfy the hunger I have inside of me for you. Yes, she is hot and so moist that I just had to taste her with my loving fingers. She longs to be opened by you and she doesn't understand why I want to give her my 3-speed virtual reality flesh feeling toy. Understanding if I do this I would want more and as many times that I get myself off me argues to want more will bother my sleep, yet the thought intrigues me so that as I stroke still sweet moist lips my hips want to respond rapidly.

"Damn she is getting so wet and my heat is rising for more pleasure but the pleasure she looks for is yours. I want you so much and I have been going to bed with you on my mind every night longing for your hands to be all over this warm body of mine. And it's driving me crazy because your sent is embedded in my memory banks and I need you right now right this instant but checking my batteries baby. Yeah, there good to go and I will take this time to release some of this pint up tension I have going on… she stops, I told you it wasn't finished. Your phone was busy earlier who was you talking too she asked curiously.

I had a lot going on with my computer and it froze and went down on me taking my phone with it, I'm just getting back on track. I'm sorry princess my badness I was calling to see wasn't it too late for you to come out.

That sounds great to me, listen let me finish up here and I'll be right over.

ELIZABETH PERKINS

Ok, see you soon princess. Antonio goes to grab a quick shower before his guest arrives, and forgets the whipped cream on the coffee table. He begins to straighten up his room before his shower he experienced a shift like his equilibrium hearing faint words (now tell you even with tears, their end is destruction, their god is in their belly and they glory in their shame, with mind set on earthly things.) the sensation of movement with feelings of transformation. No sooner than he jumped in the shower he heard his doorbell ringing like crazy. Grabbing a towel, he headed for the door, opening it he began to say do you…

Yes, I do (smiling)

Delilah!

Yes, can I come in?

I was still in my shower, come on in I'll just be a little bit.

Delilah walks into the front room and takes a seat on the couch and as she starts get comfortable, she notices a can of whipped cream on the table. Her thoughts were as curious as a cat to why it was there, she didn't say a word she waited until Antonio was through with his shower to find out. But while he was in the shower, she took the opportunity to do some investigating of her own to make sure there was nothing going on and no one that would pose a threat to their relationship. She scoured through his loft as if she worked for CSI and she was on a cold case, looking through his closets, dresser drawers and dirty clothes basket but found nothing. But she had a small vile of jasmine oil rubbing it in her hand she rubbed along the sides of his bed pillows and along the collars of his shirts and in every shoe and sneakers he had, she even marked his wallet. Invoking the four elements and chanting spirits of the elements be with me.

TEARS OF A BROKEN HEART

I beg with this token to discover the initial of my love and it harm none, so be it. She calls to the elements feeling the thick energy in the air she then thanked them for their presence there. She than found a jar in the kitchen she than breathed in it three times visualizing him and her being as one and quickly closed it and hid it under his bed far back by the leg so whatever he does it would not be disturbed. As Antonio's shower ended, he reached down and turned the water off opened the shower curtain stepped out wrapping himself in a towel and started to open the bathroom door. Delilah quickly got out of his bedroom and returned to the front room and sat back down. Antonio walked in saying; I'll just be a few minutes okay. She shook her head in agreement. Take your time love she smiled. After getting dressed Antonio walked into the front room and embraced Delilah with a warm hug. Delilah receipted her affections towards him, then picked up the wiped cream and said; whipped cream huh?

That was given to me as a bad joke at work (talking it from her) those guys are crazy down there; I'll just get rid of that (taking it and throwing it in the trash.)

Some bad joke, I tried calling you, but your phone was busy.

Oh, I was online earlier with paperwork.

Oh well I was starting to worry when your phone was busy, you know people are crazy these days. (Hugging him as she's saying) I brought a movie; I bet you thought I forgot?

You never forget never Antonio started getting things ready for dinner smoked salmon cooked in a light butter sauce, Spanish rice and sautéed vegetables for dinner, it was amazing, and Delilah was fascinated with this man she called hers. He made her feel like a princess and he her king. Being with him was like being in a movie and the script was written just for

ELIZABETH PERKINS

them. She was on cloud 9 watching him making the caramel popcorn for their after-dinner movie. Lights, camera, action!

MONDAY

Monday morning came in with the scent of breakfast in the air. Delilah was cooking pancakes, bacon and eggs, the smell of crisp bacon woke up Antonio's stomach as he opened his eyes; umm dang that smells good. He got up and went into the bathroom to wash his face and brush his teeth. Meanwhile Delilah was in the kitchen making plates and bouncing to the music on the radio. She was in a groove when Antonio walked in smiling at her. She was really enjoying the dance when she noticed him standing there, she quickly said; oh, hey... I was just... making breakfast before you...

Antonio interrupted; I see...

You hungry, I was going to wake you up but you were sleeping so well...

Antonio started picking at the bacon piece by piece; so, you in here cooking all this for me?

No, I always eat in the morning, don't you?

Sometimes not always... it's always something I have to do so breakfast is a sometime thing for me.

Well, you must learn to take some time out for yourself in the morning.

I do take time out when I get that time, having so much going on and all.

Well, you're taking some now.

That's because you're here cooking my food, so I have to eat something.

(Delilah says sarcastically) Yeah right…

They took the whole day relaxing and talking about their likes and dislikes. They played S.O.S. and joked around, a lot of laughing and playful flirting. Delilah jumps on Antonio's back as they played, he rolled her over and pins her down. Breathing heavily, she struggles to break free while Antonio taunts her; you might as well give up, you're not stronger than me… everything seemed so perfect as he looked onto her eyes, slowly he went in for a sensuous kiss. His heart began racing as he moved in closer to receive her wanting kiss, before he pulled away.

In Delilah's disappointment, she said; what's wrong?

I just want to lay net to you for a while. They lay next to each other as Delilah looked at him saying; close your eyes.

What?

It's a game, close your eyes.

(Antonio sighs) ok, now what?

Relax your mind.

(Laughing) relax my mind?

Delilah laughs with him; come on stop laughing, it's not funny…

Okay, ok (clearing his throat) ok, I got this…

You ready?

TEARS OF A BROKEN HEART

Yeah, go head (laughing softly to himself) ok I'm done… I'm done.

Delilah continues; see yourself as a little boy… think about and really see yourself… can you see him?

Yeah (smiling)

What do you see?

I was a little bad when I was young; I used to get into a lot of fights back then. I remember meeting my best friend Odo back then.

Odo?

Yeah, he didn't let anything happen to me, but he stayed in trouble. I remember when he got locked up over a bad drug deal and his brother got killed (sighing) I never understood the drug game. He sat up.

You looked up to him huh?

I did almost everything he said, but he changed, and things started changing for him.

He was like a brother for you?

You can say that… I would have done anything for him, but he didn't have his own back you know… I got older and started looking at things differently.

Wow you have been through a lot… of girls? You had a lot of girls in your life?

You mean when did I find out about sex? You're a true mess. I had a lot of girls back then but it wasn't serious then. I had this one woman I used to fight with, not hit mind you but we used to fight all the time.

What happened?

She tried to do everything to hurt me.

Things like what?

She would do things, say things and play games anything to test my feelings.

Sounds like she took you for granted.

Yeah, and she was married too.

What! Kareemah laughed...

I was given idea of being a performer from my mother's best friend, she mentioned me have I ever thought about being a dancer. Her name was Phylicia Townsend she used to work for AI DuPont Hospital; right now, she's into fitness. She used to be married to Richard Townsend he's a retired from AM Track worker, but they are divorced now. She groomed me and turned me onto her friends unbeknown to my mother. I was kicking it with all her friends, they were taking me out to dinner, and it was really nice. Phylicia took me shopping clothes, drinks, dinner it was all good! I made plenty of money just giving them what they wanted. She called me one time saying she wanted to get naked and freaky. I thought she was crazy because I never considered myself any kind of sex symbol, but after her relentless attempts though her and my mother I agreed. If I don't make the first audition, I didn't want to hear it anymore. Fortunately, I made the cut, I love the traveling the world and seeing new places.

(Laughing) You are freaky!

TEARS OF A BROKEN HEART

Man, she was crazy she said stuff like; I got some lube baby, I want to show you two things; I want you to milk in my mouth and anal.

Oh no, I was so bashful (reminiscing)

Just try it I'll show you how to be gentle with your fingers and toys.

I was like, Fingers are not other things!!

So, you won't try?

I'm not into that and I don't get the fascination.

You love me and my freaky ways, don't you? Antonio explained about the time they were caught by his mother on his 18th birthday. My mom was heated by the betrayal of her friend she would call Phylicia and ask was I at her place and she would lie to cover for me, basically for her. Then my mother called and said she was going to throw my stuff out. Because I've been at Phylicia's chilling since Memorial Day because she hit my house phone telling me to come chill with her for the holidays. Well, when I went to get my stuff. I had to call the cops for an escort. When I got there, I was every name in the book, it was nasty. The cops had to cuff my dad, so I could grab everything I could. I still left something's there, I had to go back the next day I don't want to, but I had to. It was a scary moment.

Delilah was shocked; so, she was like your pimp!

Yeah well, that was then… you want a soda or something?

So, wait, you stayed with her as in lived with?

Something like that I stayed in their guest house off the pool, no big deal.

ELIZABETH PERKINS

No big deal where was her husband what was he doing?

Why should that matter to you?

I just want to know because how do a married woman have an affair and her husband don't know it?

Antonio continued to tell his story; well, it would be during her hair day, I want you to make love to me real slow. I need it's been too long. Can you do that for me?

We don't have that much time

30 minutes sound fine for a quickie!! Are you going to meet me at the house?

No, I'm walking, you got transportation?

Yes, I'll be there at 12:00!!

That sound like a plan?

I'll come scoop you up? Where do I need to get you from? It's getting close to 12 now!

I'm on Govern Prince

Where by Van-diver Avenue?

On the corner by the park at the gulf

Ok. I'll be there about 11:50!

Ok.

TEARS OF A BROKEN HEART

We'll do the 30 minutes of hard fucking, and get you back? Phylicia tells her husband; honey I'm on my way out, but I have to drop my girl off at the hair dresser. Be back in a few.

She was a hot ass mess! Who was her girlfriend, did you fuck her?

Her girlfriend works down town I see her all the time.

What do you mean you see her all the time?

We attend the same gym.

What gym?

The YMCA

Wait a minute, wait a minute! What YMCA?

Hold on now were just friends, this is my business I have to work out three days a week because I'm an entertainer remember.

Oh, you're an entertainer; I see what you're entertaining alright. Well, who is she?

I can't tell you that because this is my job my money maker and I have a privacy rule.

A privacy rule what about all these pictures you have around your house? Is the pictures of the women with the long hair?

What women?

The women that you're talking about, this Phylicia is this her. Walking over to the photo and picking it up, is this her?

77

ELIZABETH PERKINS

No (laughing hard) that's my mother, besides I don't keep pictures of the women from the Quest here.

You never told me about her husband.

Oh, he was a yes man always doing what's best for his family; she had him in the palm of her hand. One day she called me and said; I'm going to grab a little econ-phone and txt you with the number.

What time?

What time is good for you?

I'm free remember, where we going?

I'm house-sitting for a friend she going to her daughter's graduation today. I don't know what time yet. How long can you stay out?

Not long. When she came to get me, she was right straight to the point; slow down! I go to the bathroom, and come back to this. She was all over me, a real tiger in the sack. Stop being a baby! I got tired of her and moved back home because she was controlling my life and all she wanted was sex. It was crazy she, but she kept calling and stalking me.

Damn what did you do?

I tried to ignore her, I even brought a private phone, so she can't contact me, but she found out my number; hello!!!!!!

Where are you?

At home chilling, why are you up so early on a sat?

TEARS OF A BROKEN HEART

I got my sis-in-law's car I got some running to do later? Shame you can't get away for a minute later.

I'm busy today.

I have some free time at 3:00pm met with me?

Why do you want me to meet you? I thought I said to end this.

You did, but it didn't stop you the other day now did it? While you were fucking my friends and getting paid, Bottom line, yours is over, mine isn't! You owe me...

O well, repair yours, and I'm moving on.

I knew you weren't shit, now I know why women change and go to another woman. I understand so much clearer. Maybe I'll find a girl. Maybe she'll find me! Who knows! Have a nice life, because I'm going to sure going to motherfucking try!

Damn she was crazy! Where, how did it end? Was that it?

No, she left messages like; look it's been a long, stressful week. You said you wanted to see me remember? Then you changed your mind. I made the arrangements. Was just wondering, but if I'm getting on your nerves that much, let's just leave it alone? I'll be okay! I'm just tired of people playing with my emotions. I'm just tired period! Maybe I need to move from this crazy place. People threatening to kill me it's too much! I just had to let her go man because she was stalker material, I couldn't make a move without seeing her there. But thank goodness, she moved to Baltimore, I haven't heard from her since... look I'm monopolizing the conversation you tell me a little bit about you?

ELIZABETH PERKINS

Well, I guess I'm carefree I don't worry about a lot of things, I figure if Gods not worried about it than neither am I. and if I want something I go for it…

Antonio goes into the refrigerator and start pulling out vegetables to make a salad; he gets a knife to cut up the veggies. But curious Delilah has even more questions. So, do you still have a lot of girls in your life?

No… not really, I mean I have female friends not come over anymore friends. I mean you're the only one that comes over.

Have you ever been in love Antonio?

I really don't care to talk about that.

Why we're friends, it's not like you love me right? Antonio continues to cut the veggies thinking about what Delilah just said. He was in such deep thought he accidentaly cut his finger; Aww fuck!

Delilah ran to him; oh, my let me see it! She began to suck on his finger to stop the blood. Oh, shit what are you doing? Its okay saliva is natures antibiotic, come into the bathroom baby. Antonio hated the sight of blood and peeked at it; is it bad he asked? Peeping out of one eye, Delilah thought he was cute all scared and vulnerable. He reminded her of her little brother when he fell off of his bike. Hold still don't you trust me (looking at him) I won't hurt you. Here put your finger under the water (she reassures him) you know it's not that bad. Antonio was squeamish, and his really feat strange about Delilah drinking his blood. Hold still you're in good hands, she put a bandage on his finger and kissed it all better, you're such a baby.

TEARS OF A BROKEN HEART

It could have been cut off, and what's up with you putting my finger in your mouth?

Cut off it's a mere-cut (laughing) and you were dying…

Well, it was a lot of blood, you saw it.

Yeah well, I'll finish the salad; I like finger foods, but not while it's still breathing (she joked with him) do you have some candles?

Yeah, sure I'll get them.

They sat down by candlelight and Antonio thought the night was going fine as he looked at Delilah. Her eyes seemed radiant by candlelight, taking a bite of his salad, he asked; umm… so tell me something's about you and what do you do for work... I mean while you not draining blood from unsuspecting people (he laughs to make light of the situation) are you a witch are something?

Well since you asked my family dabbled witchcraft and I know who I am as a Wiccan. I would see and talk with the spirits, at first, I was afraid but then my grandmother told me not to be afraid because the spirits in my dreams was trying to tell me something. And one night my grandfather died, and I saw him that same night and he spoke to me and touched me right here (pointing to her center of her forehead) every sense then my third eye was open. I love self hypnosis because it relaxes me, but I don't use it on people (she lied) because the energy you put out you also receive energy back in, be it positive or negative so you have to be careful with that stuff.

There are always sacrifices in life but I chose to live my life free as a bird. As all little girls that want to have it all, but keep running into so many brick walls. Me I was different I wanted the good life always. I used to play dress up and that I was a princess, put on my big sister's dresses and spinning around till I was drunk off the energy. There was nothing to stop me when I looked around the women in my family were most beautiful. My grandmother uses to say it was a cruise to be so beautiful and that modesty was the best policy for a girl like me. There was strength in being a beautiful woman. I would look at movies and see white women that was beautiful and compare my look to there's and saw that I was pretty but even more because I had color.

I was a pretty little girl with sandy brown skin with long pretty hair that never got nappy, but tangled sometimes it was so soft and curly. My mother used to dress me up with with ribbons in my hair and button up collar shirts pleated skirts baby doll socks with patent leather shoes. There was no getting dirty on her watch, she wouldn't hear of it. She was a strict single mother that worked two jobs to care for me my sister and my brothers. And in her spare time she worked for herself selling Avon and ode jobs cleaning people's homes. Our house was always clean because we had to keep house after school to earn our keep, mama said it was teaching us to keep our own houses clean when we grow up.

But I felt like a slave cleaning all the time and never getting to go out after school, so I would get lost in old Harlequin books. Books chalked full of love, adventure, romance, deceit and excitement. Aside from reading I found joy in art, I started out tracing things calling it mine, but then I took a chance on me and started drawling and creating my own work, I could do anything with a pencil and shading with tissue. I was a fast learner and I watched plenty of those painting shows that thought you the tricks of the triad when it came to art of shading. I loved old vampire movies spells and potions looking up and the differences between voodoo and witchcraft.

We believed that everything on the earth was meant to be used in some kind of way either good or bad it was up to the person that was using it. We have a long and interesting history lighting the way to the sacred; dispel the forces of darkness associated with ghosts and the dead and incubated dreams.

I grow up on words like, you can lead a horse to water but you can't make him drink? And if you pick your nose long enough it will bleed, and if you put good things in your body you'll live longer and won't grow old before your time… If you raise yourself to do better in life you won't fail yourself. If you ask for help and don't appreciate it, my grandmother says honey it will never come again. And when you burn your bridges, you've come to the end of the road.

Antonio responded; you're a bevy of information, aren't you?

Yeah, I'm a book warm. Want to hear something that relates to people but people don't want to hear it? We all are flesh eaters because we eat the dead. Killing and eating forgetting the excuses that you didn't kill the animal or mammal it has a vertebra just you and I, if we would chill out and stop all this fighting over crazy stuff like religion, that's manmade but God it's always. And if we stop telling a parent how to parent, we would be okay.

Antonio was in all to what Delilah was saying; so, can you put spells on people?

I can but…

Let me rephrase the question, have you put a spell on anyone?

Really you want to know that?

Yeah, sure I do I need to know if you're crazy or not, well not crazy but what would you do to me?

83

ELIZABETH PERKINS

For the one love I would never hurt you as she moves towards him straddling his lap. And I work at the hospital taking care of people; I'm a certified C.N.A baby.

C.N.A what's that?

Yeah, it's a dirty job but somebody's got to do it.

So, umm (kissing her) what does that Intel, this dirty job?

Well (kissing Antonio a little more passionately) cleaning up after patients basically. Checking and measuring Urinal-bags, changing diapers and colostomy-bags.

So, you're saying umm… you take shit from your patients?

Delilah laughs out loud; yeah, you can say that. They play and tickle each other; the night was wonderful and inviting. They go onto the patio and share interesting stories under the stars and the full moon. The moon seemed so close a perfect night with great conversation, Antonio couldn't keep his eyes of Delilah, she was stunning, and he spoke the words he thought he would never say to a woman; I love your eyes, beautiful smile, I could listen to you all night. And at that moment his guard was down; so, you want to watch that movie?

Let's go get it.

What did you bring?

Something scary!

Ooh

Cabin fever Delilah says in her scary voice.

I'll get the popcorn what 's it about, I can do scary movies.

TEARS OF A BROKEN HEART

You're going to love it; it's about a vicious flesh eating...

Okay, ok stop...

I know you're going to love it...

Delilah sits on the couth waiting on Antonio to pop the movie in and turn off the lights, Antonio sits down, and Delilah snuggles quickly under his arm. She exclaims; ooh this is going to be good I have chills already. Hush the movie is starting.

They watch the movie, eyes fixed on the screen and energy in the air. Antonio holds her closer eating popcorn...than after a while, Ahh! Delilah screams and jumps at the images on the screen. Digging her face into Antonio's chest, he laughs; come on don't cover your face it's the best part. Intense graphic moments with people throwing up and flesh falling of the body, people was shooting the people in the cabin, just a mess... After the movie Antonio turns the light on; that was more grouse than scary.

Yeah, I liked it when I first saw it too...

And that poor guy that thought he made it; he wasn't even sick.

Yeah, because he stayed away and only drank beer not the water, remember him and the other guy made a bet remember.

Oh yeah, he did, come here you.

What (smiling)

He slips his arms around her waist and takes a deep breath; you enjoy yourself tonight?

Yes, I did.

ELIZABETH PERKINS

So, you really want to be with me, right?

Yes, I do.

No question in your mind about that (looking into her eyes) you're positive?

Feeling the sensuality in the air she gently bits her bottom lip, he adjusts his arms a little more to hold her closer; I'm a very private person and I like my space... but I'm willing to share, I don't like complications and ugh, you want to mess that up (smiling) probably with the possibility of more to come. He kisses her warningly.

Delilah says; you know this could get emotional, I'm not predictable and I'm not perfect.

Okay, I'm not looking for perfection, and sine we have this commitment thing going on there is something I need to tell you.

Already what?

You are such a beautiful woman, with a wonderful personality, I think you will have me so hooked on just your essence, that I won't be able to look anywhere without seeing you in everything. You actually make me feel very special in just this short time... And I have never felt special to anyone my entire life. And I mean never... I have always just been an option; you have never looked at me like that. For that, I deeply thank you... Come sit down.

What is it?

Okay something happened the other day and I think you should know about it.

TEARS OF A BROKEN HEART

If this is about, Antonio cuts her off; just let me say this with no interruptions because I'm feeling kind of guilty about it for not telling you. He takes a deep breath and explains himself; remember the whipped cream on the table?

Yeah?

Well, an old friend of mine stopped by before you got here, it was nothing. I told her to leave and that's where the whipped cream came from.

Delilah was surprised; oh, are you still…

No, nothing like that she doesn't even live in Delaware she moved a while ago. She is visiting her peoples and she just happened to stop by, things where finale a long time ago.

And you're just telling me no, I don't understand why?

Because if you're going to be a part of my life than you should know the truth. I don't like games and I want you to be my woman.

Delilah was delighted; I appreciate you telling me that. She looked at him through curious eyes; no other guy would have done that. I will give you so much pleasure baby I just want to get my hands on your wonderful body. I want all the man you posses within you and more. I not only want to make love to your body but also your mind so that every time you get hard you only think of me, your real woman that will love you for this life time. Yes, you are my man baby I don't care about the other women as long as your heart is mine.

I am in love again, for the first time in so many years, and I have to say, it feels so damn good. I feel the joy and excitement of a child at Christmas, the heat and passion of a high school freshman, and the well-being and confidence of a young adult.

ELIZABETH PERKINS

At this stage of my life, one could say that there are those who wish they were in my shoes. But as delightful as that may be, a man should never lose sight of truth...it could mean the difference between extreme bliss and total disaster emotionally. He should always keep a small measure of sound reasoning in place, because despite all the joyous feelings of love, all the pangs of desire, and all the fire of his passion, especially where there is a particularly beautiful young woman is involved, there will always be apprehension.

There is absolutely no better feeling in the world than when a beautiful young goddess falls into your life and all of a sudden makes you realize exactly what has been missing all this time. All that time, wasted...you ask yourself, where has she been all this time? But it's all good, though, because you've professed your feelings as eloquently as your vocabulary would allow. And she responds favorably, too, which raises your levels to usually unreachable points.

There are, however, three very big hurdles a man must overcome before he can be at rest with his overjoyed heart, and unfortunately, at least one of those hurdles is unattainable. First, because this young lady ("young" being the operative word in this case) is so attractive and so popular, he would be foolish to think or believe that he is the only one to have these feelings for her, and just as naive to think that he is the only one in whom she could possibly have interest. The odds are almost never in his favor, given his own limited circumstances.

You're not like anyone I ever knew. You inspire me to think in high-definition color as opposed to black and white...having such joy in my life has prompted me to open up the vault in my heart and gleefully share its contents...

I your words are sheer poetry as I drink in every understanding of you. I'm so taken by your mind that it's ashamed to have such apparition yet to feel so unworthy of all

TEARS OF A BROKEN HEART

your sweetness. But I'm ever so humbled by you Delilah you are extraordinary loved me queen. Come now I have to get to you home now and I'm tired.

Delilah responded softly; yeah, me too, but I just hate sleeping alone.

Antonio smiles; than you can stay here with me sleeping… only sleeping.

They lay in each other's arms taking in the value of the evening Antonio was affected by Delilah's very presence. Stroking her hair with his fingers he could smell the hint of coconut that emanated from her hair. His eyes closed as Delilah snuggled in and together vanished in their sleep.

Tuesday came in softly with Antonio laying awake looking at Delilah sleeping capturing her essence in the new sunlight. He couldn't get her out of his head, and he tried to stay focused but; rise and shine, show me those beautiful eyes. Dreams last night of holding you close as you slept. Playing with your hair and cuddling through the night just for me to wake up from my dream of it all. You're so amazing. I played with your hair and ears the whole night. That was so fun to hold you and have that moment. I'm going to be smiling all day. Delilah wakes up hearing him whispering such beautiful words of love for her. Antonio replies; hey sleepy head.

Good morning.

Listen I have some time off and I was wondering would you like to go to Hershey Park with me.

Oh, my goodness, really!

Yes really?

ELIZABETH PERKINS

Oh no, I can't… I don't have any money.

Look don't worry about that I asked you to go with me, not do you have any money. And another thing, if you need anything let me know alright? I'm your man so I don't want to hear what you ain't got okay.

Delilah smiled with delight in his take charge dominating ways. She answered; yes, when are we going?

Thursday morning.

What about your job?

I told you I'm off, I don't go back until next Thursday.

Oh, really Delilah moves in closer; umm I got to go love, I'll call you later alright?

Alright kissing her softly; you be careful okay; you have a man that is waiting to see you pass through that door again, okay?

Okay baby, I have to go home and get myself together, time waits for no one. He walks her to the door as she kisses him good bye.

Delilah rushes home to tell her friend Alisha about Antonio; hey girl I'm just getting in from my date last night with Antonio, what's good with you?

You know how it is with those crazy people at the job but all in all I had a good day at work just home relaxing. I do have a question if I am not being too noisy, how did you and this Antonio end up together?

TEARS OF A BROKEN HEART

I met him by chance the day after the show, she lied. He brought a young teen into the community center that he found on the street crying. Turned out she ran away from home. So, since then he has been such a great person, calling to check on her and things.

Oh, wow he sounds like a great guy; he did a wonderful thing for the young teen I hope she is alright.

Yeah, she is but that wasn't the first time she had ran away and because of reoccurring events she was taken from her mother and placed in a home. He has been a pretty good friend and I was thinking about doing whatever I could to make him mine. But alas, we shall only ever be friends. From what he tells me But, we won't spend all our time talking about him. That would be weird but just know that I would never want to see him hurt. He has a very soft heart for a man in this day and age.

I see…! Were you going to keep things under wraps until now? At least he told you already you must be a good friend.

Yeah, he is a good friend, but I need to know I will feel safe with him being I have a hard time trusting men. But from what I know of him I'm finding my heart wanting to be with him, you know. But I have no intention on hurting him at all Alisha keeping this between us girls I'm not ready to tell him about that yet.

My mouth is closed. You have my word.

Thank you, Alisha you are a good friend.

Now what are you guys planning?

Nothing we're just enjoying each other.

ELIZABETH PERKINS

Nothing wrong with that I'm jealous, you found a great man, and he has a sexy ass delicious looking woman.

I'm excited about him Alisha and he does have a sexy quality to him, I'm just glad he is all mine.

Well, I am glad that you found a man like him. There are so many of us that would pass him by, for the other guys that keeps us wet from how they look or act. I was like that most of my youth, and went from pretty dog to pretty dog. And I think that's what made me become bisexual. I got tired of getting dogged by men, and when I wanted a decent one, they didn't want me because of the attitude I had developed. So, please treat him good. Be that woman that he needs and deserves.

I will, Alisha I promise he is in good hands with me girl. And I understand how you feel I once had a woman in my life I was in love with but because of her career she moved away from me. I didn't tell Antonio that because I knew he wouldn't understand, how do you tell a man that? But I am so happy with him, you know it's funny I never thought I would meet my potential husband like this but you know I'm really feeling him and it feels so good.

You would be surprised to what men would understand these days. I'm not sure if you have realized it but he seems very wise and probably has seen a lot in his field. Besides, you may not believe it but I'll tell you something I don't think you guys have discussed. Dancers have pretty much dated nothing but bisexual women. But that's not hard considering that today, most women are bisexual. So, I am sure he would not have an issue with you being bisexual. Not many men do as long as you are not sleeping around with women behind their backs (laughing) I made a joke. But for real, if you do mess with women, never leave your man out if he is a good man. That's one way to run him off.

TEARS OF A BROKEN HEART

I feel you Alisha, I will tell him because he should know everything about me. And your joke was funny I'm still smiling, I'm glad we're friends I don't have too many friends because people are judgmental you know. And you are right men are a trip I seen men that tell me in not dark enough. And I struggle with my complexion all the time; it's a trip feeling like I don't fit in anywhere.

Struggle no more beautiful, it seems like your guy has only one thing he is into and that's a woman that act like a woman. I think you have made a good impression on him.

I pray I'm enough for him, but I intend to keep him happy always.

Why do you feel you are not enough for him? That's the first thing you have to get over. Never doubt yourself because then you will start to doubt your man.

Yeah, I know, but he is so well renowned to the world and so travailed. I just want to make him happy and pray he is not color struck because to me a black woman is a black woman you feel me. He is a man that will knock me off my feet and I'm starting to feel him inside, you know. Antonio is everything I want in a man, usually men want me because of what I look like but not Antonio, he just wants me.

Men like to see what they do for a woman, and know that the woman likes it. I don't think he is color struck and your skin tone is beautiful girl. Most men would love to be in his shoes when he touches and kisses it, and I know he will because that dude is a freaky ass guy, come on girl he's a stripper!

I feel you on that (laughing) trust me I'm ready, but we're going to take it slow first (laughing).

That makes me warm inside seeing a couple blossoming.

ELIZABETH PERKINS

You're a beautiful friend Alisha no one understands a women's heart like you do.

Flirting with me, are you? I might have to come have a threesome if I'm not careful.

(Laughing) you are a mess I love it Alisha: talk with you later girl…

On this trip to Hershey Park, they stayed at a bed and breakfast that was an old brownstone. After a restful night they awoke the next morning and ready for an enjoyable breakfast. The server who waited on them was an elderly black woman with a thick southern accent. Who graciously served Antonio his juice, coffee and toast, but when it came to Kareema she through the juice in her lap and broke the tea kettle on the floor next to her?

Furious over this inexplicable behavior, Antonio stood and up and demanded to know what the outburst was all about. The server ignored him and glared at Kareema and screamed a curse: "God is going to get you!" she shrieked, then threw down her apron and ran from the building. Antonio complained to the management. The management that promised to fire the woman, but they claimed she could not be found. Fortunately, the management gave them their entire stay there for free. They leave for the park to try to forget about the incident and have some fun in the park. Woooooh...! The ride comes to an end Kareema said: that was fun...!

Yeah, that ride was crazy!

Oh, can we get on that one?

Where?

TEARS OF A BROKEN HEART

Come on they go get on every ride the park had to offer, with all the excitement they can stand. The games Antonio was a gamer and he knew how to play almost every game in the park, he even won Kareemah a real big bear that looked like a lion and she named him (Lionel) thank you baby…

Come on let's go to the chocolate factory. They towards the chocolate factory passing all the fun rides they previously were on earlier. They go inside the factory and instantly the wafting of the chocolate aroma filters their senses… Umm that smells so good Kareemah could hardly control her tongue to speak.

I know, it's like your compelled to gorge yourself in some chocolate, look at the cocoa beans.

Just imagine they make chocolate out of that little bean.

Are you hungry?

Yeah, I could go for something sweet. They go and stock up on popcorn balls, cotton candy while also picking up photos of them on the rides. Before they head back to the Brownstone, once they arrived a message from the owners were even called in to apologize exceedingly for their recent employee's horrible behavior. Antonio looks at Kareemah asking well that was nice of them, hey princess did you enjoy yourself today?

I had a great time thank you (she yarns and stretches a little) excuse me baby…

You lie down and get some rest love…

Kareemah lies down to get some rest and before her head hit the pillow she was swept up in a dream. She was out helping a friend out when two men started arguing, one was across the street and the other was standing on the other side of the street which happened to be right next to her car. The argument started heating up over a bad trade when the man in the red car went to his car and opened his trunk pulled out a large weapon and started firing. People started running and so did Kareema when the shots were spread into the block, shooting the people running and Kareemah was hit three times. She felt the burn of the bullets as they penetrated her body and she could feel the coolness of blood began to drain out of her body. The open holes of flesh in back legs of her and shoulder, and she was on the ground gasping for breath. When he saw she was still moving he came up on her putting the barrel of the gun to her head as she reached up and felt heat of the barrel of the gun on her head. Kareemah started reciting Psalm 23:4 Yea, though I walk through the valley of the shadow of death, I will fear no evil; for you are with me; your rod and your staff, they comfort me, over and over again. The man hesitantly backed away got in his car and drove off. She was dying, and her eyes began seeing apples growing out of the ground quickly, not apple trees but apples growing whole, up in bundles in the mud; they were so red and they were piling up in the quickly in the mud while she started calling for Antonio over and over again and her eyes opened at 7:59am.

Over the next few days seemed to have its effect on Kareema, she lost her purse along with $300 cash, her credit cards and her I.D. The lights refused to stay lit in their bedroom and bathroom, while the rest of the Brownstone lights worked fine. She was haunted by horrible demonic nightmares the entire time she was there; and swore up and down that she had been awoken several times during the night to find the server standing over her watching her. Finally having enough, she talked Antonio into cut the trip short and returned home. But many incidents of misfortune seemed to follow her for an entire year.

Antonio turns on the television to catch the news. A 19-year-old man was killed, and four other men were wounded in

TEARS OF A BROKEN HEART

a shooting spree in the Bronx yesterday, the police said. They were shot on a street about 4 p.m., said a spokesman. The two victims were taken to Lincoln Medical Health Center. The 19-year-old was pronounced dead on arrival said a hospital administrator, the other man was shot in the foot and was in stable condition by evening. The other three victims suffered gunshot wounds to the legs and drove themselves to the Hospital where they were in stable condition as well said a hospital administrator. The police were investigating whether the shootings were the result of a feud.

After getting dressed Antonio turns off the television to go meet with Kareemah he was ready to get a place and settle down with her, he knew she was the one for her. You seem like you are a pretty well put together woman. Are you an affectionate woman? Or do you hate touchy feely?

I am very affectionate but at home because I don't want to disrespect any children that may be watching me. Children see everything and are impressionable I want to be that role model as well for them as well. Not kissing and rubbing on my man all outside, you know people need respect of not only person but children too. That's why our teens are run amuck today.

Very understandable princess... And I agree... once they see grownups kissing all in public, they will be out there doing the same. Except they are not prepared for the outcome of what it leads to, but as long as I get to kiss you on a vacation at an all-adult resort, I'm good (laughing)

That sounds good to me...

I'm always good princess, all the time, and at everything I do... I can prove that to you...

(Smiling) as long as you do what you do with only this Princess there is nothing to prove.

97

ELIZABETH PERKINS

Oh, trust me; I'm a one-man woman.

Wow that makes a girl smile.

You are a woman... very far from a girl princess and I'm just the lucky one that caught your attention. Hope I can keep it.

You are the only one that admires me love and believe me women get tired of it men hollering at them and when you respectively just say hi and keep it moving they act like they don't understand not interested, or you got to be the B word.

But what makes me so special that you would go against your "not looking at other men" to consider being with me?

I think you are my make, you fit me. Remember I'm not an image I'm a person just like you love.

Yeah, but the gorgeous women always try to date the gorgeous men... and I'm just average... so I feel a little undeserving of your attention when I think about it. I guess I have some issues to work through with that.

I'm not so gorgeous I have flaws too, am just your run of the mill average woman. I have seen women more beautiful.

The waitress came over to see if we needed anything, more to drink or dessert....

(No thank you we're fine) Antonio continued: You are perfectly flawed though sweetie. And even women with flaws are more sought after by men than there are men with flaws. Such is reality, women tend to go more about looks than personality, and men tend to go more for body or sexuality than face or personality. But I would rather have a woman that makes me feel at ease with who she is, than one that gets attention

TEARS OF A BROKEN HEART

based on how she looks. But you have both... so I got to get my mean on when guys come around you (laughing) I am set on having a big house, warm weather and you beside the pool enjoying your life with me. I'm going to make you mine... Wow it seems funny that I want to be with you like that already, and we don't even know if we are truly compatible yet... But I'm hoping... I was afraid to love but I have never been a quitter and I would love to make you the one that gets my heart, mind and all the love that I have yet to be able to bestow on a woman. Because by the time I turn around, I am being betrayed... So, please don't hurt my heart...

I have been in relationships that I didn't feel safe in because the men were weak and I'm a siesta that needs a strong black man in my life. One who will be there for me when I'm weak because I do have a fear of being around people (men) as my past haunts me so (don't want to talk about it) But that is why I have a fear of men in large numbers and my fear of the night. I won't hurt you Antonio if whatever hurts you hurts me and I'm not having any of that.

I know all too well about betrayal and a heart so broken it disintegrates and blows away like the wind. Tears that soak the pillow so bad that you can't even sleep on it, yes, I know all too well. I will guard your heart as if it was in my own chest, the only way you can get it back is if you cut it out and I know you wouldn't do that because that would hurt you and you wouldn't do that to you. I love strong just know that.

Well, I will do what it takes to protect my woman at all times. Even from herself or her indulges if they can harm her. When you feel comfortable, I would love for you to tell me why you are afraid of the night. But if you don't want to talk about it, I will understand... listen before we head out... I just want to say, "If we were living together, we would be in bed, cuddled up, kissing and touching as we listen to the crackle of the rain hitting the window" I want to all of you and every bit of what you want me to have. Hey, you want to check for a hotel around here or are you spending the night with me...

I'll spend the night with you if you behave.

Behave in what way? The first night I plan for us to have a long talk, cuddle and see how that feels I may (more than likely) kiss you or give you a long massage. Antonio called for the waitress and paid the check

At home Antonio cuddled with Kareemah till she fell asleep. He didn't sleep at all that night he was up in his own thoughts. (I'm brave, but of you I am afraid. Your beauty (inside and out) is incomparable by far. Your words bring joy, giggles and a smile to my face. Yet my heart race at the mere thought of touching your face. In the morning I will be here and allow you to judge and decide our fate. While you lay in bed sleep yet missing your king, I am awake and desiring a queen. We have similar thoughts; we share similar ways... Yet I find myself asking what is it you find so good in me? What could a lowly man like myself possibly have that brings out your desire? There is nothing greater than pure love, but for my life, it has been something that has eluded me. I have long thought that my heart would never feel such joy as I see other non-worthy men receive. Men that dog women cheat on women and still those women flock to them because they are utterly handsome or have money. I am nothing more than a mere stick of grass in a forest full of oaks.

What could I possibly offer to a woman that is desired by a multitude of men? I find myself wondering this all day and late at night. I wonder if for you, I could really be Mr. Right...If we are to be together, trust me, I will shout it to the masses. Just know that while you lay there, sleeping like an angel, you have an angel thinking about you, God watching over you and love aimed at you. I want you to smile every time you think of me; every time you think of you and every time you think of us. I'm not the richest man around, and I have lost so much dealing with bad women and bad choices in women. I can only offer you me, my love and the chance at a happy future. I hope that's enough for you, because you are more than enough for me.)

Early that morning Antonio slipped a ring on her finger while she was still asleep. When she awakes, he was sitting in a chair on her side of the bed. She looked at him saying: what's wrong baby?

He answered: well, I was wondering would you keep that ring on your finger for me?

She looked at her hands saying: what! Oh baby…! Yes, yes, yes!!!

I want to be the good man in your home baby…

My home…?

I have been thinking about you since I first saw you princess. Not one day goes by that you are not on my mind... no matter how busy or stressed I get, you cross my mind and I smile... just at the thought of you.

Awe baby that is so sweet I been thinking about you as well. And I love the way you think on me and I think of you always as well. Never think you are out of my mind because you are not. You are my center always.

Another thing Princess, I need to know this before I get up and sign this lease. I found a 2 bedroom/1 bath house for a little fewer than 800 a month. I'm trying to make sure you are comfortable with things like that before I commit myself to a lease. And are you ok with 2 bedrooms? Or would you rather just have a one bedroom?

ELIZABETH PERKINS

Wait why can't you just move in with me love?

It's different for a man you know. We have to have everything if we expect to make a woman comfortable... A man moving in with a woman and he has nothing, a poor excuse for a man. So, we already have the living room suite, I still have two more pieces to buy for my bedroom set... I'm getting a big screen TV after thanksgiving (They are cheaper then) So, I got my 37 inches right now.

Okay but why such a big television baby.

For movie night baby...

Oh okay...But we have to go with caramel popcorn.

Of course, and a blanket or a big air mattress to lay on the living room floor and cuddle up. I don't want to limit cuddling to just the bedroom... so we have to make every room to where we can cuddle and enjoy it. We will need to get a bedroom suite for the second room in case we have family over sometimes...

I know just what to get for the room, I will handle that myself.

Good, because that is the woman's territory in a house... You pretty much decide on what comes in, and how it's decorated... and who is allowed to come over... I'm the king of the castle, but the Queen dictates a lot of the house type business...

I know that's right my King we will conquer the world together always.

Ok my caramel queen... Let's go get some breakfast.

You mean lunch…

TEARS OF A BROKEN HEART

They get dressed when Antonio says: we should get married somewhere in Aug, we will take us a 7-day trip. So, that gives us 9 months to save up about 4,500 dollars to spare for a trip. It doesn't cost that much, but having some money to do a little shopping wouldn't hurt. A 7-night cruise to the Bahamas would cost just fewer than 2,000 dollars and would stop at two ports in the Bahamas... but making love on a ship would be wonderful... That is something I have never done before... Let me know what you think and what you want... I will stand by you, support you and love you completely princess. You are my destined wife; I will do my part and we should be able to take that trip and I will make it so!!

Baby anything that saves us money sounds fine with me, wow you are so good to me 7 days sounds great I would love to go anywhere with you.

Are you sure you are into me that much princess?? You know we will have some disagreements sooner or later... bad habits will come out sooner or later...

I know all relationships come with disagreements every relationship has them give me another one.

I might be too freaky for you, and I'm just trying to make a living like everyone else. Just because I'm an entertainer does not mean anything it's just a job baby. I see why the stars say it's lonely at the top and money doesn't make you happy. And I haven't reached that far yet and people are starting in on me, but I'm about to make changes soon as I pass the Bar.

You know people will want to know you for different reasons. In the beginning, I wanted to know you because of your dancing. Of course, it was your banging ass smile that made me feel like we could be more. I thought you didn't want to see me anymore mainly because I figured you had far too many women that looked way better than me pursuing you.

ELIZABETH PERKINS

But after we actually talked, and you confessed that you were really single... I started to see you as a handsome man that was down to earth and simple living than any man I have come across in all my years... And that started me (very fast) to wanting to know you in a romantic way, to develop a strong loving relationship with you... And I am glad you gave me the chance.

As I lay on the table, I could hear the doctors talking and working on my body my arms are extended parallel to my body, with my legs extended and relaxed. I must say that this experience was quite unsettling to say the least. I could hear everything that was being said and done. There was a tube down my throat and the medical staff did not have an oxygen mask on my nose. They were taking pulse ox and blood pressure with urgency. They were working just above my pelvic area and the muscles in my stomach was being pulled apart and the presser of something being tugged at. I could feel the cool of the instruments inside my body and fingers moving things around. The doctor was clamping this and that, when suddenly I heard someone say: I'm losing her pulse doctor she's flat lining!

Everyone started moving quickly and talking so fast that I didn't realize, they were talking about me. The doctor listened to my heart for about one minute and feat for my pulse for another; I realized He was examining me. My whole life flashed in front of me, from that moment backwards to segments of my life before. The review was not like a judgment at all. But it was passive, more like an interesting moving video of what was being played before me. I was still aware of motion and being moved into a room and soon everything was quiet. I felt tears streaming down my face, when one of the nurses blotted the tears from my face and covered me with a white sheet.

The silence called to me as I opened my eyes. I had a 360-degree peripheral vision of the whole area around me. But not just in the room I was in, but beyond my room. I got up from

TEARS OF A BROKEN HEART

the table and started towards the door, as I opened the door, I heard voices but saw no one. I headed for the waiting room to get my husband, and as I walked, I saw my surgeon talking to two police officers. That was strange I thought as I passed them by I noticed that they didn't seem to see me at all. And my husband was not in the waiting room, so I went outside to look for him. It was raining a strange cool rain that didn't seem to find me as I walked in it. And soon there sitting in the car alone was my husband; he seemed to be sad for some reason. I got in the car setting next to him and said: what's wrong baby?

He never answered me, so I reached out to touch him and that's when I realized I was dead. And I thought: was this it, I mean I didn't feel anything. I'm setting right here. What do I do now? My husband slowly started the car and drove away from the hospital. He drove in the rain in his science. I could tell he was thinking about something. I could always read his face but never told him that. I watched him drive our car home park like he always does and hesitantly go inside. He walked upstairs and found his way to the closet, where he fiddled around until he found a black leather back memo binder.

That held all of our important information that we only used when we were going to talk with our insurance company. Wait how long have I been gone; time means nothing here. I don't remember him coming to look at me or set down by my side, I don't even recall he's tears of sorrow and grief. What else will I forget in this realm of nothingness. I pondered the situation as I paced back and forth in the room. I couldn't over stand the meaning of being here. Was this a waiting period until something came to collect my new form, what was this new image of me. I thought the bathroom and I was there already looking at the mirror and that was all I saw. I was energy moving through matter and I felt nothing but love and comfort.

But what of my dear sweet husband, he was now all alone without me, who would take care of him now that I was, what was I? I went back to the room, but my husband was gone! Where did he go? I heard faint voices coming from downstairs, my husband and his brother were sitting and talking about a terrible car accident involving a container truck traveling to fast and the driver that had a heart attack behind the wheel that hit my car... My car! My visions of bright lights and a truck going too fast for road conditions, as the truck crashed into her car and the car hit a three-foot-high ridge of oiled gravel and flipped into a series of violent somersaults. As she was catapulted through the front window before the car smashed into a ditch. I was suffocating in that moment.

Oh my god I was killed in that accident! I thought about the hospital for some reason and I was there dying. Feeling torn between two worlds wanting to remain on earth while at the same time feeling a strong pull to unite with this strange light. But something or someone was crying out to me, pulling me towards them. This was it I thought, I didn't have a chance to say goodbye to anyone! Then I saw her, this tiny little baby girl with tubes in her nose, mouth and IVs stuck in her ample little arms. She was so very helpless and weak.

She barely had a pulse and was struggling to breathe with a pattern very rapid breathing and then periods of no breathing. In short terms, her heart was weak and overworked, making her body want to hyperventilate and, subsequently, there is no more energy to breathe for a period of time. Her organs were getting less blood and, thus, less oxygen. Without oxygen, the cells in the organs begin to die, then the organs die and finally she would die. She needed me, she needed my energy and strength and I needed her to breathe and live for her father. So, I reached down into the little protected crib that they had her in and held onto her until we submerged into one being. My spirit felt warm and celestial inside this new host, as my spirit slowly moved into hers. I saw a light and wanted to go into it. The light was like a circular opening that was warm and bright, but there in that moment I knew the answer. I closed my eyes in that bed and when I opened them, and I was standing in the most beautiful tunnel of light I could ever describe.

And I instantly knew I was where I belonged. Negative feelings and emotions were gone; it was as though all knowledge had been instantly downloaded to my being. As I continued towards the light, I saw the image of a 2-year-old little girl laughing and playing and I felt intensely moved by her. My spirit could not contain all the love I had for her. When I looked back down at her, I recognized her as my daughter.

BRANDON'S WORDS
JULY 20, 2016

Me and my wife have been studying life after death all day. Did you know that science can't explain consciousness or emotions? Did you know a baby does not become aware of its existence until 5 months after birth? Physical pain and emotional pain stems from two different areas. The making of all things is energy. Sleep is the closest thing to death because it only takes 10 seconds to pass out from the loss of oxygen to the brain which at that time...you die. In deep sleep or a comatose state...you lose consciousness and are no longer aware of your existence. Regaining consciousness means to become aware of your existence. This tells me that when you die... you don't know that you're dead. Out of body experiences tells that you can leave your body and become aware outside of the body which would also mean that you still live after death. What do you think?

Brandon & Williaeshia Holmes

THE WAVES OF MISSING YOU

I was out shopping for my Thanksgiving/ 50th birthday party in 2017. Going with the none traditional Thanksgiving a wave of missing Brandon my son hit me, and I couldn't stop crying. This would be my first Thanksgiving without Brandon. The wave was so strong I was overwhelmed, and the flood waters came with uncontrollable abundance. As I fought through the storm of tears, I asked my husband to talk to me and help me through. I couldn't tell you what he spoke with me about, but suddenly the storm subsides and the evening goes on. After while I find myself on Facebook scrolling along and I find myself captured by a live feed of a tattoo Artist.

He was good, I mean his art was amazing putting art to skin. John was filming doing and awesome job and his commentary was on point. Soon I found myself in a conversion with John about the Artist. Soon the Artist began speaking and again I'm in communication with them both. And it was about my son, mind you I never said his name, but the Artist said he was doing pitchers of loved ones lost. I spoke about Brandon and wanting to get a photo done of him, so I can have him with me always. I continued to watch the live feed until it started freezing on me. So, I decided to go to bed early that night. I could see beautiful was tired as well and soon I was falling asleep. Dominique was dealing with the children; they were running around the house. We were house setting for my uncle somewhere, it was strange. But some purple friends of nine were there and Prince's music was the topic of conversation. But beautiful was lying next to me, dressed mind you.

TEARS OF A BROKEN HEART

He was about to leave when my phone started to ring. It kept ringing, so I reached for it and saw my son's photograph on the phone... Hesitantly I picked it up, hello? The caller asked to speak with Brandon. I hung up the phone. This woman kept calling for him. I didn't understand why she would call me asking about my son that passed. And soon I grow tired of her calling and decided to share this with my daughter. Dominique began telling me she called the girl and told her she spoke with Brandon. He was alive, and he was still with us. I couldn't believe it, I started asking: where is he? And meanwhile my phone kept ringing. I told the caller to stop calling this phone. But she kept calling me, so I told her, look Brandon's not here and if he was, he wouldn't want anything to do with why she was calling him for. I started ignoring the ringing of my phone. Then things started braking around the house and I couldn't figure out why. Then Asia said Daddy is doing it on accident. I looked as my granddaughter and told her stop saying that. I looked up and Brandon walked in the room with a radiant smile full face and high cheekbones, saying Hi momma.

He hugged me, and I felt his heartbeat his body mass, he felt so strong holding me. And I held on to him in hailing his sent like I did when he was born. It was Brandon, it was my son! His voice rippled through me with a rumble in his chest like only he can speak. Then I rubbed my fingers through his lushes' beautiful black curls. And I cried Brandon, where were you? Do you know what I been through! He said but I'm here now Mama, I'm always here with you. He smiled at me as I said I miss you, Brandon. He said I missed you too mom. And I woke up thinking I miss you, Brandon.

Leasia

Elizabeth Perkins

Williaeshia & Brandon Holmes

HE LEAVES BEHIND

HIS DAUGTHER LEASIA NEVE NICOLE HOLMES
HIS LOVELY WIFE WILLIAESHIA HOLMES
HIS FATHER CURTIS HOLMES JR.
AND
HIS MOTHER MARCHELLE E HOLMES
TWO BROTHERS GERALD W DORSRY
CURTIS HOLMES III
TWO SISTERS DOMINIQUE S HOLMES
CAPRICE L HOLMES
TWO STEP DAUGHTERS
STEPFATHER AMIYN PERKINS
STEPMOTHER NICOLE HOLMES
A HOST OF NIECES/NEPHEWS/AUNTS/UNCLES AND FRIENDS
HIS GRANDPARENTS
ALICE E WALKER AND GERALD WALKER
HE IS PROCEEDED IN DEATH BY HIS GRANDPARENTS
CURTIS HOLMES SR AND CAROLYN R HOLMES

Brandon & his princess, Leasia

www.ingramcontent.com/pod-product-compliance
Lightning Source LLC
LaVergne TN
LVHW020414070526
838199LV00054B/3608